## "Maybe we should go in."

"Maybe we should," Neil agreed.

But instead of doing that, he slid his fingers along her throat, tilting her head ever so slightly. He slipped those fingers into her hair a little at a time.

And then he slowly inclined his head over hers. And then his lips met hers.

Just like that, time stood still as the kiss between them blossomed and grew until it couldn't be measured in any breadth and scope that had been invented yet or even made any sense.

Ellie's mind stopped protesting, stopped attempting to put the brakes on.

Instead she allowed herself to be wildly, breathlessly swept away down an uncharted river she had never even imagined in her wildest dreams existed.

Rising up on her toes, she slid her arms around his neck, felt herself responding to the heat of his body. Not just responding, but suddenly finding herself wanting more.

Eagerly.

Where had this come from? And why, in heaven's name, now?

And why with a man who couldn't possibly want to stay in this small town once his job was done?

**FOREVER, TEXAS:**
**Cowboys, ranchers and lawmen—oh my!**

Dear Reader,

Well, here we are again, back in the world of Forever, Texas, where everyone is into everyone else's business and if they're not all one big happy family, they still really do care about one another. So much so that when one of their own, Miss Joan, appears to be having serious health issues, the town's community becomes exceedingly concerned. Dr. Davenport gets in contact with Neil Eastwood, a well-known, innovative cardiac surgeon who, despite his discipline, has grown dissatisfied with his life and is searching for some sort of meaning. Once Dan tells him the problem he's encountered, Neil decides to come out for a visit. Who knows? Maybe he'll find what he's looking for in Forever while helping his friend with Miss Joan.

Elliana Montenegro has lived in Forever all of her life and she dreams of having her own small airline service and flies a small plane. Since Forever doesn't have an actual airport, Ellie is dispatched to bring the good doctor to Forever. There, Neil soon locks horns with the stubbornly uncooperative Miss Joan, who is very much in denial about her medical condition. Totally focused on this task, neither Neil nor Ellie realize that they are also falling for one another.

Come, read and see how this all turns out. Oh, and if you still have some doubts about investing your time reading this latest story about the citizens of Forever, I can promise you a surprise. Miss Joan's estranged younger sister, Zelda, surfaces to further complicate matters.

As always, I thank you for taking the time to read one of my stories, and from the bottom of my heart, I wish you someone to love who loves you back.

All the best,

*Marie Ferrarella*

# Secrets of Forever

## MARIE FERRARELLA

HARLEQUIN

**SPECIAL**
EDITION

# HARLEQUIN®
## SPECIAL
## EDITION™

Recycling programs
for this product may
not exist in your area.

ISBN-13: 978-1-335-89485-4

Secrets of Forever

Copyright © 2020 by Marie Rydzynski-Ferrarella

This edition published by arrangement with Harlequin Books S.A.

For questions and comments about the quality of this book, please contact us at CustomerService@Harlequin.com.

Harlequin Enterprises ULC
22 Adelaide St. West, 40th Floor
Toronto, Ontario M5H 4E3, Canada
www.Harlequin.com

Printed in U.S.A.

*USA TODAY* bestselling and RITA® Award–winning author **Marie Ferrarella** has written more than two hundred and fifty books for Harlequin, some under the name Marie Nicole. Her romances are beloved by fans worldwide. Visit her website, marieferrarella.com.

Visit the Author Profile page
at Harlequin.com for more titles.

To
Lucy,
Who knew that 37 pounds
Could tear around the house like that?
We're exhausted, but our hearts
Are smiling!

Thank you, German Shepherd Rescue Society of OC
For bringing Lucy into our lives

## *Prologue*

While Miss Joan's Diner—the only restaurant in the small but thriving town of Forever, Texas—was rarely ever empty, the hours between 11:00 a.m. and 2:00 p.m. were hands down the busiest time of the day. That was usually the time when ranchers and small business owners chose to take a break from their hectic lives and reconnect with friends and neighbors. For the space of an hour or parts thereof, they forgot about deadlines and schedules, or the problems that ranching might generate, and just paused to take a deep breath.

Even so, most of Miss Joan's patrons were usually in a hurry, wanting to eat and go before their self-indulgences created some sort of a problem that left them answerable to either bosses or, on occasion, to themselves.

Miss Joan, owner of the diner for as long as anyone could remember, presided over all this organized chaos with an iron, blue-veined hand, making sure her customers never had anything to complain about, be it the service or the food.

As usual, her full complement of waitresses—four—was on hand during this time frame. While they knew better than to rush her customers, Miss Joan always made sure they kept everything moving right along.

Noticing one of her regulars staring off into space while cradling a cup of coffee in his rough hands, the sharp-tongued woman said, "You want to nurse what's in front of you, Jefferson, go to Murphy's."

Murphy's was the local saloon run by three brothers. When they'd taken over the family establishment after their uncle died, the Murphys had struck a deal with Miss Joan. They'd promised not to serve any food other than pretzels, and Miss Joan had promised not to serve any sort of liquor, not even beer. It was an arrangement that served both establishments well.

Today, for some reason, it seemed as if the diner was even busier than usual.

The noise level was higher. Not to mention the diner seemed hotter than usual. Miss Joan could feel perspiration beading along her brow beneath her ginger-colored hair. She paused just for a second to take in a deep breath.

Something felt off to her and she didn't like it. She just wasn't herself.

The diner owner had just refilled Jerry Walker's coffee cup and turned to replace the coffeepot on the burner when she abruptly froze. Her perspiration intensified. Not only that, but her pulse raced in time with her heart. The latter was suddenly beating so hard, her head felt like it was spinning.

Isolated in her own little world, Miss Joan didn't see one of the waitresses closest to her, Vanessa Aldrich, looking at her, concern etched on her fresh features.

Vanessa had temporarily forgotten about her customer sitting at one of the tables, waiting for his rare steak.

"Miss Joan?" Vanessa whispered. When she received no answer, she repeated the diner owner's name and laid a hand on the older woman's bony shoulder.

Miss Joan all but jumped the way a person did

at the sound of gunfire. "What?" she snapped, doing her best to try to cover up her reaction to what was the most startling moment of physical weakness she had ever experienced.

"Are you all right?" Vanessa asked her.

Miss Joan had prided herself on being equal to and surviving every curve that life had ever thrown at her, including one very big one. Surviving and managing to go on even stronger than before. It was a well-known fact that Miss Joan was the one who provided strength to many people in Forever. She did so while maintaining an air of wry aloofness.

Despite this façade, in times of need or trouble, Miss Joan was always the first person everyone turned to, the first to provide unspoken moral support, not to mention the occasion roof overhead and/or source of much needed employment. It was an open secret that the woman had a heart of gold even though she pretended to remain distant and disinterested even when interacting with her patrons.

The terrifying wave of weakness disappeared as suddenly and mysteriously as it materialized and, within moments, it was as if that debilitating moment had never even happened.

Almost back to her old self, Miss Joan drew

back her thin shoulders and raised her head like a soldier on the verge of battle.

"Of course I'm all right. I'd be even better if my waitresses were moving a little faster instead of stopping to gawk at the woman they work for. Your break time comes *after* the lunch rush, not in the middle of it," she reminded Vanessa as she waved her hand at the man sitting to her right. "Now take Rudy here his steak before it turns cold and Angel has to make him a new one."

"Yes, Miss Joan," Vanessa murmured, hurrying over to her neglected customer's table.

"The girl was just concerned, Miss Joan," Rick Santiago, Forever's sheriff, pointed out to the woman he had known ever since he had been a boy. "There's no need to snap her head off."

Penciled-in deep brown eyebrows drew together over the bridge of Miss Joan's amazingly perfect nose. "There's *always* a need to bite their heads off," she informed the sheriff with no hesitation. "And I'll thank you to let me run the girls in my diner the way I see fit. I don't tell you how to run the town, now do I?"

The sheriff merely smiled because they both knew that was not the case. Miss Joan was the most opinionated person Rick knew. He also owed her a great deal. Everyone in town did. He nodded at his almost empty coffee cup. "How about a refill?"

"As long as you promise to keep your opinion to yourself," Miss Joan said. She positioned her coffeepot over his cup but held off pouring as she waited for Rick's response.

He nodded. "For now," he replied.

Miss Joan sighed. "I suppose that'll have to be good enough. For now," she echoed as she finished refilling his cup.

Rick inclined his head in silent agreement. A draw was the best that anyone could hope for when it came to Miss Joan.

## Chapter One

Miss Joan raised her eyes as she straightened the sugar dispenser on the counter.

"If you're expecting me to sprout wings and fly away, you're going to be disappointed, so stop watching me like that," she ordered Cash, her grandson thanks to her finally tying the knot with Harry Taylor some years ago. Making her way over to Forever's other lawyer, one look at Miss Joan's face told everyone within sight of the woman that she looked as if she was loaded for bear. "Don't think I don't know what you're up to," she all but growled, her hazel eyes pinning Cash where he sat on the stool.

"And just what is it that I'm up to, Miss Joan?" the tall, blond-haired young man asked her innocently.

She didn't like playing games. Miss Joan's eyes narrowed like two laser beams as she looked at Cash. This sort of attention made her feel feeble.

"Don't play dumb, Cash. It doesn't suit you. We both know that old man sent you here to watch over me. Well, you're wasting your time, not to mention a perfectly good seat in my diner." Miss Joan nodded at the stool. "A seat a paying customer could put to good use."

"When it starts getting crowded in here, Miss Joan," Cash promised her, "I'll vacate it."

Miss Joan snorted. "Don't you have any wills to write up or update?" she asked, then added, "And I don't mean mine."

Cash laughed. "You're going to live forever, Miss Joan. Grandpa just wants to make sure that you're healthy while you're doing it," he told the town icon with a smile.

Miss Joan cleared away an empty cup left behind by a customer. "Humph. You want to waste your time, you can go right ahead and—"

The lanky woman's words seemed to dribble away as a really sharp, intense pain suddenly stabbed her in her chest, bringing with it a wave of heat accompanied by a weakness she found herself incapable of dealing with.

Miss Joan couldn't seem to catch her breath.

Because she had abruptly stopped talking, Cash glanced up. He immediately saw the change in Miss Joan's face. As usual, he was wearing a suit, but that didn't even begin to stop him. Cash instantly vaulted over the counter to get to her side, managing to acquire a dollop of whipped cream on his trousers as he did so.

He reached the woman just as she looked as if she was going to sink to the floor.

"Miss Joan, what's wrong? Are you having a heart attack?" her grandson asked, putting his arms around the thin, shaken woman as Ruby and Laurel, the two waitresses currently on duty, quickly closed ranks around the diner owner.

Ruby, the older of the two, spoke first. "Get Miss Joan some water," she ordered as she looked at Laurel.

Miss Joan barely heard the young woman, or Cash. They were just noise. Shaken, she was focused on what was happening to her—and frightened. The heated wave had already started to pass and, while not entirely releasing Miss Joan from its death grip, she was doing her best to rally.

Becoming aware of their hands attempting to

hold her steady, she waved away the waitresses as well as her stepgrandson.

"I'm fine," Miss Joan insisted then snapped, "Stop fussing. I'm fine, I tell you." She straightened like a regal queen.

Cash withdrew his hands and released the woman who still appeared to be very fragile to him. He remained close to her.

"No," he told her firmly, "you are *not* fine. In case you missed the message, your body is putting you on notice, Miss Joan, and you're going to listen to that warning, do you understand?"

When he looked as if he was about to take hold of her again, Miss Joan shrugged him off. "What I understand is that Harry raised a grandson who doesn't know how to behave respectfully around his betters," she fired back, deliberately avoiding the word "elders" because she felt it reflected poorly on her.

Cash Taylor was known for his easy-going disposition, but he drew the line when it came to being bullied. "Nonetheless, I want you to go see Dr. Davenport."

Miss Joan was aware that every eye in the diner was on her. She definitely didn't care for this sort of attention.

"*You* go see Dr. Davenport. I don't have the

time," she declared, turning her back on Cash and moving away.

"*Make* the time, Miss Joan," Cash told her in a no-nonsense voice.

Miss Joan slowly turned around and glared at the young man. "If I make the damn appointment, will that get you off my back?" the woman demanded, her tone far from friendly.

Cash's eyes met hers. "Yes," he answered in no uncertain terms.

Frustrated, Miss Joan blew out an impatient breath, a player conceding the game under duress.

"Fine!" she snapped. "I'll make the appointment!"

"That's my girl," Cash said affectionately, planting a kiss on Miss Joan's shallow cheek before she could pull her head away, out of his reach. He knew that Miss Joan wouldn't say that she was making an appointment if she didn't intend to live up to her word. He considered the battle won and went to tell his grandfather.

As good as her word, Miss Joan did, indeed, make the appointment.

The problem was, Cash found out the following week, that Miss Joan hadn't *kept* the appointment. He discovered this when he'd called Forever's lone medical clinic to ask when he could pick Miss Joan up.

The clinic's head nurse, Debi, informed him that Miss Joan had called to cancel the appointment set for later that morning.

Stunned, Cash told the nurse that he was "uncanceling" Miss Joan's appointment and to expect her within the hour. Hanging up, he strode out of his office, disappointed and annoyed.

"You're not really surprised, are you?" Olivia Blayne Santiago, his senior partner, as well as the sheriff's wife, asked when he gave her the update. "Miss Joan never listens to anyone except her own little inner voice."

Cash shook his head. He refused to accept this turn of events. "I just came in to let you know I'll be out of the office for the next hour or so."

Olivia eyed him knowingly from her office chair. "You're going to force Miss Joan to go see Dan, aren't you?"

Cash looked utterly determined. "Even if I have to carry her there myself to do it."

Olivia appeared skeptical. "You might be biting off more than you can chew."

Already on his way out, Cash stopped just short of the doorway. "If anything happens to that woman, I'll have two funerals to arrange, and I'm not up to dealing with that. I'm not ready for that old man to leave me yet," he added bluntly in case there was any question about whom he meant.

Olivia glanced at her calendar. There was nothing pressing on it this morning. "Do you want me to come with you?"

"No, I'll handle it. If any of my clients want to talk to me, ask them to call back this afternoon," he told her. Then he added, "And maybe cross your fingers while you're at it."

Olivia smiled warmly. "Makes holding down the fort a little tricky."

"If anyone can do it, you can," he told the attractive brunette as he left her office.

"Are you taking an early lunch?" Miss Joan asked when Cash entered the diner.

"No," he said, walking up to the counter where she was currently standing, "I'm taking a stubborn grandmother to her appointment at the medical clinic." Cash frowned at the woman. "I'm disappointed in you, Miss Joan. You broke your promise."

Miss Joan raised her chin, a prizefighter spoiling for a fight. "I did not," she informed Cash indignantly. "I promised you I'd *make* an appoint-

ment with Davenport and I did. I did *not* promise
to keep it," the woman pointed out.

Miss Joan never ceased to amaze him, he
thought. The woman could wiggle out of anything.

"The way I see it, you have two choices, Miss
Joan. You can either walk out of here with me on
your own power, or I can carry you out. Either
way, you *are* seeing the doctor."

Miss Joan's eyes darted to her waitresses and
then to the sheriff, who had stopped by for a
quick cup of coffee before heading out to the El-
liot Ranch to handle a local dispute.

"Don't look at me, Miss Joan. I'm on Cash's
side," Rick protested.

Miss Joan's face clouded over although, deep
down, she hadn't expected the sheriff to answer
any other way. "I'm not going to forget this."

"As long as you're around to carry a grudge,
that's all right with me," Rick told her. "We're all
worried about you," he added.

Word had spread fast about how pale Miss Joan
had turned the other day, not once, but twice. No
one wanted to witness a repeat performance.

"Listen to me, you two," Miss Joan all but
growled. "I am fine." Her tone was crisp, measured. Then she repeated the word—*"Fine"*—with
emphasis.

Rick was unmoved and remained seated, nursing his coffee. "We just want to make that official and have the doc tell us so."

"So, which is it, Miss Joan?" Cash asked. "Are you going out on your own two feet, or do I have to carry you?"

Her eyes flashing, Miss Joan muttered a few choice words under her breath as she took off her apron and tossed it on the counter. She knew when she was defeated.

"On my own two feet," she said coldly.

Cash nodded. "Good choice."

Miss Joan gave it one more shot as they walked out of her diner.

"Davenport's a busy man, boy. I don't like taking up his time like this over nothing," she cried.

Cash wasn't buying it. "Attending your funeral will cost him more time," he quipped, escorting the woman to his car.

"Since when did you get so dramatic?" Miss Joan asked.

Closing the passenger door after her, Cash rounded the hood and got in on his side.

"It comes with the territory," he replied. "The sooner we do this," he told her, starting up his car, "the sooner it'll be over."

Miss Joan crossed her arms before her small chest, unwilling to buy into his narrative.

"You don't have to hang around," Miss Joan told her grandson as they walked into the medical clinic. He hadn't left her side since picking her up at the diner.

"I'm afraid we have a slight difference of opinion when it comes to that matter, Miss Joan. You might as well save your breath," he said kindly. "I'm staying."

"This is harassment, you know," she snapped as they entered the semi-crowded clinic. There wasn't a single person there she didn't know, but Miss Joan avoided making any eye contact. She was much too angry to do that.

"No, this is insurance," Cash replied mildly as he nodded at Debi, one of the two nurses sitting behind the reception desk. "I'm ensuring the fact that you're going to be seeing the doctor."

"Dr. Davenport is waiting for you, Miss Joan," Debi said, rising and coming around the desk. "If you'll just follow me."

"Do I have a choice?" Miss Joan asked tersely, glancing over her shoulder at Cash.

"No, ma'am," Debi replied, doing her best not to

smile at the situation. She knew the older woman wouldn't appreciate it. "You do not."

Miss Joan shook her head in disgust. "And to think that I gave this town the best years of my life," she complained, grudgingly walking behind the nurse.

"We'd all like to think that those are still ahead of you, Miss Joan," Debi told her as she led the woman into the rear of the clinic. "You're in exam room one," she said, gesturing toward the room.

It was obvious that Dr. Daniel Davenport was waiting for her, eager to resolve this as quickly as possible. He owed the diner owner a debt because of the way she had treated his wife before they were ever married.

"Hello, Miss Joan," Dan said warmly, taking her hand between both of his. "I promise to make this as painless as possible."

"It's already too late for that," the woman informed him. "Look, I'll save us both some time and trouble. I've had a couple of heart flutters. Nothing serious, but everyone overreacted and made a big deal out of it, including that old man I made the mistake of marrying. Now, I've got a diner to run, so if we're through here—"

Dr. Dan gently took Miss Joan by the arm and led her over to the examination table. "No, Miss

Joan, we are not through here. I need you to sit down on this table and let me examine you."

Annoyed and stymied, Miss Joan exhaled dramatically. "Oh, all right. Just make it quick," she instructed impatiently.

Dan smiled into the older woman's eyes. The lined face of a warrior, he couldn't help thinking. "I'll make it thorough."

Miss Joan scowled, far from happy, but she knew that resistance would only prolong the process, and she wanted to be gone. "Let's get this over with," she ordered.

Helping Miss Joan onto the exam table, Dan flashed a smile at her. "Your wish is my command, Miss Joan."

"Ha! Don't push it, sonny," Miss Joan warned the physician.

It took a lot for Dan not to laugh.

"So, are you satisfied?" Miss Joan asked, buttoning up her blouse. She never took her eyes off Dan. "I assume I can go now, right?"

He made one last notation in the woman's exceptionally thin file. To his recollection, Miss Joan had never been inside his medical center since he had first reopened it.

"No," he answered. "And yes."

Impatience creased Miss Joan's lined forehead. "I'll go with 'yes,'" the woman said, slipping off the edge of the exam table. She turned toward the door.

"I thought you might," he said and then dropped his bomb. "I want you to see a specialist."

Miss Joan raised her eyes accusingly. "I just did," she pointed out. "You."

"No," he contradicted. "I mean a cardiac specialist."

"Forever doesn't have a cardiac specialist," she reminded him tersely.

"No, it doesn't," he agreed, "but—"

"Well, that settles it, doesn't it?" Miss Joan announced. "I can't see one if we don't have one. Now, I've got people waiting for me, so if you don't mind—"

"Oh, but I do mind, Miss Joan," Dan said, catching her gently by the arm and preventing her escape. "You have a big heart, but it's a heart that clearly needs help, and I'm not qualified to do the type of surgery that you need." He watched as shock passed over the older woman's face. "There're some fine cardiac specialists in Austin—"

Miss Joan shook her head, vetoing the idea before it was actually even spoken.

"Unless one of those 'fine' doctors is willing to make a house call to Forever to see me," she informed Dan, "I'm afraid this idea has run its course. So, if you'll just step out of my way, sonny, we can both get on with our lives."

Dan shook his head. "You are definitely one stubborn lady, Miss Joan," he said.

"I never claimed to be anything else, sonny." Her features softened slightly. "Look, I appreciate the corner my grandson and husband just painted you into, but you did your best. You gave me an exam—not that I wanted one—and you gave me your opinion, which I duly noted. Now let me get back to what I do best—"

"Being stubborn?" he asked wryly.

"Being useful," she countered. "Send your bill to Harry," she said, straightening her blouse. "So maybe next time that old man'll think twice before having me practically abducted."

But Dan wasn't ready to give up. He recalled a conversation he'd just had with one of the doctors he had gotten to know well while interning in New York. Back before he had ever come out here and gotten hooked on Forever.

"What if I could get one of those cardiologists to come see you?" Dan asked just as Miss Joan reached for the handle on the exam room door. "If he came here, would you see him then?"

Miss Joan laughed shortly, thinking the chances of that happening were slim to none. Mostly none. She turned around to look at Dan with what passed for her own version of a broad smile on her thin lips.

"Sure, if you can get one to come all the way to our little town to make a 'house call,' then yes, I'll see him—or her. After all, I'm nothing if not reasonable," she told him with a cackle. And then she looked from Dan to Debi, who had remained in the room for the examination. "Now, am I free to leave or do you have an armed guard posted outside this door?" she asked.

"No, no armed guard, Miss Joan. You're free to leave," Dan told her.

Something about the expression on the doctor's face told her this wasn't over yet. But if she pressed the issue and asked, she was fairly certain it would escalate into a bigger discussion, and she had no time for that.

She had people waiting for her at the diner. Probably a lot of people by now.

## *Chapter Two*

Maybe it actually *was* time for a change, Dr. Neil Eastwood thought.

Admittedly, change had been in the back of his mind for a while, ever since his conversation with his old friend, Daniel Davenport. He had felt this restlessness building up inside him for some time but now it seemed to be coming to a head. Neil knew that if he said as much to some of his friends and the colleagues he worked with, they wouldn't hesitate to tell him they thought he was crazy.

Here he was, a skilled cardiac surgeon at the top of his field, associated with the best, most re-spected hospital in New York City—the city that never slept—and all he could think about was leaving it all behind and starting over somewhere else.

Quite honestly, the feeling had taken root even before he and Judith, his now ex-fiancée, had broken up. But the breakup had definitely escalated this desire for change.

Although she'd adamantly denied it when he'd called her on it, there was no denying the fact that Judith had wanted to orchestrate every minute part of his life. At times, he was still surprised that she hadn't attempted to elbow her way into his actual practice, telling him which patients she thought he should see and which he should turn away.

Judith had made it clear that she'd thought he should only minister to patients who could pay handsomely for his services. Namely *rich* patients. That way, his reputation would continue to grow and he would be able to take on patients who would pay top dollar for his services, no matter what he wound up charging. Judith Monroe had very expensive tastes and although her family certainly had money—old money—she was of the opinion that one could never possibly have *enough* money.

Neil, on the other hand, had not gone into cardiac surgery for the money. Oh, he had to admit that, for a while, it was seductive, almost alluring, to be paid for what he loved doing. But the concept of financial reimbursement had all changed in one night. He'd been doing back-to-back shifts, one of which had been whimsically referred to as the "graveyard," when an ashen-faced father ran into the ER carrying his five-year-old daughter in his arms and screaming for help.

As luck would have it, Neil, the only doctor on duty at the time, turned out to be instrumental in saving that little girl's life. A little girl who would have died if not for him. The exhilarating feeling he'd experienced when she'd finally opened her eyes had been unbelievable. He'd known then that he wanted to recapture that feeling again and again.

He'd also known that such exhilaration wouldn't be possible if he continued to dance attendance on the rich and famous, monitoring their lab tests and adjusting their medications just so they could continue eating and drinking to excess while partying with their friends.

In retrospect, that sort of life, the life that Judith had wanted for him, all felt so meaningless and utterly empty.

He needed his life to mean something, needed his existence to make a difference, the way it had when he'd treated that little girl. He had actually brought her back from the abyss. By all rights, she had been clinically dead for almost five minutes.

Neil thought of that little girl as his miracle child. When she'd opened her eyes and "come back," somehow, miraculously, there hadn't been any brain damage whatsoever. He had personally tested her for symptoms because he couldn't believe it.

He'd taken that "miracle" as a sign that he needed to shift the path of his life. He needed to dedicate himself to something more worthwhile than what he was doing.

When he'd told Judith about his midnight epiphany and the path he was contemplating taking—operating on patients whether or not they could pay at the time—it had been the beginning of the end for the two of them. Judith had accused him of being crazy, which was immediately followed by a knock-down, drag-out verbal assault where she did the bulk of the railing, not to mention vicious name-calling. She'd called his sanity into serious question, as well.

When that hadn't made him retract his words, she'd played her ace card. She'd threatened to leave because, under no circumstances, could she see herself "shackled to a loser," which she maintained was what he would be if he followed through.

Instead of her rant causing him to "see the light" the way she had expected, Judith's threat had only managed to accomplish his sudden exposure to an invigorating, tremendous sense of relief.

It was as if a huge weight had instantly been lifted off him. No grief, no shock, just a feeling of sweet relief.

He was suddenly free to do whatever he wanted with his life—all he had to do was figure out what that was.

That was when Fate stepped in, Neil thought now, in the form of a phone call.

In his apartment, located a few prestigious blocks from the hospital, he was contemplating his next move, as well as life without Judith, when his cell phone rang. He debated letting it go to voice mail, then changed his mind. He didn't want to put anything off anymore. Whatever was out there, he intended to meet it head-on.

Picking up his cell phone and swiping it open, he announced, "Eastwood."

"Neil?" a deep, familiar voice he couldn't quite place said on the other end of the line.

"Yes, but I'm afraid you've caught me at a disadvantage—"

He was about to ask the caller to identify himself when the person on the other end did just that.

"Neil, it's Dan. Dan Davenport," he added unnecessarily since they had just spoken less than a month ago.

"Oh, wow!" Neil cried. "Funny you should call. I was just thinking about you and the way you had just taken off for that small town to continue your brother's practice. You said it was just until they could find a replacement for him. How long did you wind up staying?" Neil asked, intrigued and amused by the whole thing.

Dan laughed softly. "You know the answer to that, Neil. I'm still there."

"Do you have any regrets?" Neil asked. As he remembered it, Dan was the one who'd had the most detailed plans for his future out of all of the interns. And then his life had taken a sudden, unexpected, detour.

"No, not a single one," Dan answered honestly. "Actually, that's what I'm calling about."

"Not having any regrets?" Neil asked, slightly confused.

"No, about doing the most worthwhile thing with my life that I never initially planned on doing."

Neil experienced an eerie feeling that he was suddenly standing on the edge of the rest of his life.

"Go on," he quietly urged.

"I need your help, Neil," Dan began, warming up to his subject. "There's this venerable old woman in Forever who runs the diner here. It's the only restaurant in town."

As a born-and-bred New Yorker, Neil couldn't envision a place with just one restaurant. "You're kidding," Neil marveled. "Just how small is this place?"

"Small," Dan assured him. "But size doesn't have anything to do with it." He paused for a moment, regrouping. "This would make more sense if you were here, which is what this phone call is actually about. Miss Joan—"

"Miss Joan?" Neil interjected. "Is she a delusional Southern Belle from another century?" he asked, amused.

"Miss Joan is definitely not delusional. It's what everyone around here calls her and it's actually a sign of respect. Anyway," Dan continued, not wanting to keep Neil any longer than he had to, "Miss Joan has developed some cardiac issues. From the exam I gave her, I'd say she probably needs an angioplasty, or possibly a stent put in, or an ablation." Aware that meant burning away some tissues in the heart, Dan conceded, "My experience in these procedures is rather limited and I'd prefer having a specialist look at her to determine the necessary course of action."

*So far, this all sounds logical*, Neil thought. "So what's the problem?"

Dan gave it to his friend in a nutshell. "We don't have a specialist here in Forever."

"Then have someone in her family—I take it she's not a spring chicken," Neil guessed.

Dan felt it was rather a cold way to assess the woman, but since he was asking for a favor, this was not the time to chastise his friend. "Not really."

"Have someone take her to a specialist," Neil concluded.

"That's the problem," Dan admitted. "Miss Joan claims she's too busy and she won't budge. So I asked her if she'd be willing to see a doctor if the doctor came to see her. I managed to get a grudging 'yes' out of her. Personally," he admitted with a laugh, "I think she doesn't think I'll find anyone."

*No mystery there*, Neil thought. "I'd say she's right."

*Here goes nothing*, Dan thought. "I heard via the grapevine when I talked to Wayne Matthews—" a neurologist they both knew "—that you're looking to relocate."

*That is only partially true*, Neil reasoned. "What I'm looking for is to find a purpose."

Good enough, Dan thought but didn't say. "Well, while you're looking, maybe you could come out here on what I'd consider to be an errand of mercy."

Since Neil wasn't trying to stop him, Dan talked quickly. "Miss Joan is the heartbeat of this town, provided that her heart keeps on beating, of course. If you can come out and give me your professional opinion about her condition, I can personally guarantee that you will have approximately five hundred people eternally in your debt."

"Five hundred people, huh?" Neil repeated, amazed. "Is that how many people there are in your town?" he asked incredulously.

"Yes. Give or take," Dan added.

Neil picked up on the phrase and put his own interpretation on it. "I take it that a lot of people are leaving."

"You'd think," Dan agreed. He'd been guilty of thinking that himself once, but he'd been wrong. "Actually, these days there are more people coming to Forever than leaving. Since I came here eight years ago, more people have moved here than have moved away.

"Anyway..." Dan returned to the reason he had

called his friend. "The problem is, we still don't have a hospital here," he confessed. "So, what do you say? Do you feel like doing a good deed and having everyone in town think of you as a hero?"

Neil laughed. "You know, Dan, I don't remember you as the type to exaggerate. Is that something that comes from living in Texas?"

"No, and I'm not exaggerating. Listen…" he went on, "I'll pay for your ticket and you can stay with Tina and me and the kids when you get here."

Neil read between the lines—or thought he did. "Translation, there's no hotel in town, right?"

"As a matter of fact, there is, and it's a few years old," Dan told him. "I just thought you might like to experience what it's like to *live* in Forever. Hotels are pretty impersonal."

"But you do have one?" Neil questioned, wanting to know just how primitive the town actually was.

"Absolutely," Dan assured his friend.

Neil paused, thinking. "Well, I do have a lot of vacation time stored up." He had been working almost nonstop for a year, taking on extra shifts at the hospital when he wasn't at his practice. "It might do me some good to get away for a while."

"Fantastic! When can you be here?" Dan asked.

Neil looked at the calendar on the wall that dictated his life. There was nothing on it that couldn't be handed over to one of his fellow specialists. "When do you need me?" he asked.

"Yesterday."

Neil didn't detect a smile in his friend's voice. "Is it that serious?"

There was a short pause while Dan was likely thinking of how frail Miss Joan had looked when he'd examined her. More so than usual, though he avoided giving Neil a direct answer to his question. "To be very honest, I'd rather have her examined sooner than later," he told Neil. "Okay, you make the arrangements to fly out, give me the exact details and I'll pay for your car rental when you land."

"Car rental?" Neil questioned.

"I'm afraid so," Dan said. "There's no airport in Forever. You'll be flying into Houston and then driving from there to Forever."

"Uh-huh," Neil replied. "Just one small problem with that plan," he said.

"What?" Dan asked.

"I don't know how to drive," Neil told him.

Dan had difficulty hiding his amazement. "You never learned how to drive?"

"I'm a New Yorker," Neil stressed. Learning to drive had never been a priority to him. "You remember how great the public transportation system is in New York, not to mention we have all those cabdrivers. And now we have all those other independent services practically everywhere you look. The city is crowded with them. There's no need for me to learn how to drive a car."

"I suppose I can see your point," Dan conceded. He had learned to drive because he liked his independence and didn't like waiting for buses and trains, but admittedly that was a personal choice. Dan thought of the patient he had seen just last week for a routine checkup to renew her pilot's license. "I think I might have a solution. Let me make a call," he proposed. "Meanwhile, you do whatever you need to do to get ready to come out here. And, like I said, the sooner, the better."

This was going a little bit too fast, Neil thought. "If I come out, it doesn't mean that I'm staying," he warned, wanting there to be no misunderstandings about the matter.

"Understood. As far as I'm concerned, you're just coming out as a favor to me—and to enjoy a change of scenery," Dan said. "I really appreciate you doing this, Neil."

"Hey, that's why we became doctors, right?" Neil asked. "To make a difference."

That was the way Dan felt now, but it wasn't

what had motivated him to enter medical school to begin with. "Actually, I initially became a doctor because I was hoping to land a position with a prestigious practice and have an excuse to play a lot of golf." Dan chuckled at the man he had once been. "Man, I can't tell you how glad I am that that didn't work out for me. All right, give me a call with all the details when you're ready to come out. I promise it'll definitely be worth your while," Dan concluded.

"Sounds good to me," Neil replied. "I'll talk to you as soon as I get everything in place."

"Count on it," Dan promised.

Neil ended the call, a bemused expression on his face. Funny how things sometimes arranged themselves. Less than a decade ago, he, Dan and Dan's brother had finished up their residencies and were on the brink of launching their medical careers. Of the three of them, only Dan's brother had set his sights on a town in Texas that, from what he had said, was apparently badly in need of a medical professional.

Forever had once had a small medical clinic, but that had closed its doors thirty years prior to their graduation. All set to go there, Dan's brother had agreed to one last night of celebration before leaving for Texas in the morning. Dan had been the one to persuade him to come along and had been driving the car back from the restaurant. Alcohol hadn't even been involved, at least, not where Dan and his brother had been concerned.

The driver that had plowed into them, however, had a blood alcohol content that was over twice the legal limit. He emerged from the accident totally unscathed. Dan sustained several injuries that had landed him in the hospital and his brother had wound up in the morgue. Grief stricken, Dan had decided to take his brother's place in Forever until another doctor could be found to fill the position to be Forever's new medical professional.

Eight years had gone by. Neil assumed that his friend had stopped looking for someone else to take over. He knew that inertia wasn't responsible for Dan still being there. He had to admit that he was more than a little curious as to what had managed to take a man who had clearly had his eyes focused on a lucrative practice to change his mind and allow himself to be won over by a town that contained barely five hundred people.

This was definitely going to be a change, all right, Neil mused. And if nothing else, it would do him some good. This trip would either reinforce this new mindset of his—or it would "bring him to his senses," the way Judith had shouted at him when she'd seen that he was having doubts about the path his life was taking. It had been her attempt to get him back on that path.

Flying down to Forever would allow him to reconnect with a man whom he had once regarded as being one of his best friends.

New York born-and-bred, Neil had never been outside of the state, nor had he ever had any desire to be. This promised to be very interesting.

And, he thought, it would give him the opportunity to make that difference he had been craving to make. That was if he could talk the iconic "Miss" Joan into listening to what he had to say.

If Dan was right, that was definitely going to be a challenge.

Neil smiled to himself as he placed his suitcase on the bed and opened it. He had always liked a challenge.

## Chapter Three

Adelyn Montenegro shook her head as she watched her older sister check over her fifteen-year-old Piper Meridian passenger plane. The plane, which Ellie had bought secondhand from Arnie Crawford at a bargain price—and was still paying off—when Arnie decided to retire from his aircraft service, was housed in what had once been a barn. With her grandfather's help, Ellie had converted the barn into an airplane hanger. It seemed to Addie that her sister spent an inordinate amount of time fussing over the old plane.

"I swear, Ellie, you baby that old hunk of tin as if you were involved in a relationship with it."

Addie brushed her straight, midnight-black hair out of her eyes. "Don't you ever get tired of it and just want to go out and have some fun?"

"Leave your sister alone, Addie," Eduardo Montenegro, their grandfather and sole guardian since they were five and seven, chided. Ellie flashed him a grateful look and he smiled at the more industrious of his granddaughters. "I have always taught you girls to follow your dreams and this plane is part of your sister's dream."

"No, Pop," Ellie corrected the gray-haired rancher who, in her opinion, worked far too hard and too long each day, running their horse ranch, "it's just *part* of the beginning of my dream." She stepped back, wiping her hands on the rag she had been using to clean part of the plane's wing, and examining her work. "Someday, I'm going to own a fleet of passenger and cargo planes." She saw her sister roll her eyes at that. "Or at least double what I have now."

Addie sighed. She loved her sister but, in her opinion, there were times when Ellie behaved more like an old woman than someone who was twenty-six years old. "Well, just remember what happened to Amelia Earhart," Addie warned.

"The point is, even *you* know who that is," Ellie said. "And that says a lot."

Addie frowned as she shrugged. "I know who you are, too, but that doesn't do you any good now, does it?" she quipped.

Ellie opened her mouth to send a few choice words in her sister's direction, but Eduardo decided to cut in before this escalated into a real squabble. He loved both his granddaughters, but he had little to no patience for arguments.

"Girls, girls," he said sternly, "if you have all this spare, leftover energy for arguing, maybe you can put it to good use and help me with the horses this morning. They need to be fed, and both Billy and Luke are busy with other chores," he said, referring to two of his ranch hands.

Addie looked crestfallen. She knew there was no arguing with her grandfather when he took that tone. "Yes, Pop."

Ellie, however, couldn't agree to go along with his request. "I'm afraid you're going to have to count me out, Pop," she apologized. "I promised Dr. Dan I'd swing by the medical clinic this morning."

Ever since his son and daughter-in-law had suddenly been taken from him as a result of a car accident, leaving him two little orphaned girls to raise, Eduardo had become keenly in tune to anything that might mean his suffering any further loss.

He looked at Ellie sharply. Was she ill? "What's wrong?"

"There's nothing wrong, Pop," Ellie assured him. "The doc said he just wants to talk to me."

Addie thought it was just her sister looking to wiggle out of chores. "You know," she said to Ellie, "I hear they've got these newfangled things now called 'telly phones,'" she told Ellie. "You pick up a receiver, dial a number and it's like the person's right there in the room with you, talking into your ear. Maybe you could try that," she suggested, catching the tip of her tongue between her teeth.

Ellie gave her sister a dismissive look. There were times when Addie could really get on her nerves. "He said he wanted to talk to me in person. Is that all right with you?"

When Ellie told her that, even Addie looked slightly concerned. "Well, that can't be good," she speculated with a frown. Her eyes swept over her sister. "You feeling okay, El?"

"I'm feeling fine, thank you." She spared both her sister and her grandfather a look. In her grandfather's case, it was to put him at ease. "As a matter of fact, my last check up at the medical clinic had all my tests come back next to perfect."

"You, perfect?" Addie questioned, trying to

cover up the momentary display of concern that had slipped out. "That can't be right."

"Very funny, wise guy," Ellie said. She knew exactly what her sister was trying to do. "Anyway," she said, turning toward her grandfather and doing her best to put his fears to rest, "the doc said he had something to ask me and he wanted to do it in person." She turned to her sister with a big smile. "But Addie here can help you with anything you need. Right, Addie?"

Because their grandfather was still right there, listening to every word that passed between them, Addie couldn't answer Ellie with the retort hovering on her lips, begging for release. So instead she was forced to say, "You can count on me, Pop— even if you can't count on Ellie."

Eduardo's waist had grown slightly wider over the years and his once thick, jet-black hair had grown partially gray at this point. By all accounts, he was still a handsome, virile-looking man more than equal to the task of dealing with his ever-squabbling granddaughters. Each of them in one way or another reminded Eduardo so much of his spirited late son. In a way, it was as if James was still there, he thought, but he couldn't be seen as taking sides in any dispute.

"That's enough, Addie. I know I can count on

both of you, each in your own way. Now, stop wasting time squabbling. Ellie, go see what's so important that Dr. Dan has to see you in person instead of just telling you what he wants over the phone."

"Yes, Pop," Ellie said, hurrying out of the makeshift airplane hanger.

"And, Ellie…" he called after his granddaughter as she left. "If this does turn out to be anything serious, I want you to call me immediately," he told her. "Do I make myself clear, young lady?"

"Yes, sir—and it won't be," Ellie promised just before she picked up speed on her way to the house.

"Didn't you once say that the good die young?" Addie reminded her grandfather. Like Ellie, Addie was protective of the old man, not wanting to cause him any undue concern. However, there were times when she couldn't help herself. "That means that Ellie's gonna live forever, Pop. There's nothing to worry about."

Eduardo sighed and shook his head, his thinning mane of gray hair moving in the autumn breeze as he frowned to himself. On the one hand, dealing with his granddaughters kept him young. On the other, he had to admit that the back-and-forth confrontations were tiring.

*I'm too old for this*, he thought as he heard Ellie's Jeep engine start up. The constant refereeing was wearing him out.

Ellie, in her Jeep and driving toward town within minutes, had to admit that her curiosity had definitely been piqued. Forever was an exceptionally friendly town where everyone knew everyone else's business. But this was the first time that Forever's doctor, the man officially credited with reopening the town's medical clinic after thirty-some odd years, had ever asked to speak with her in person.

Although she never wanted to cause her grandfather any worries, what she had told him was true. She had just recently had her annual physical for her pilot's license. The results had proclaimed her to be better than all right. She seriously doubted the doctor had made a mistake or overlooked something. He was far too thorough for that sort of thing. Nor would he have knowingly exacerbated her concern that something was indeed wrong by playing any sort of game.

So then, what was this all about? she wondered. No two ways around it, Dr. Dan had definitely aroused her curiosity.

She pressed down harder on the accelerator.

When Ellie walked into the medical clinic, the reception area was crowded as usual. But the moment she crossed the threshold, Debi was instantly on her feet.

"Come on in, Ellie," she said by way of a greeting. "The doctor's been waiting for you. He's with a patient," she told the younger woman. "But he asked that you wait for him."

Ellie glanced at her watch, a graduation gift from her grandfather. Because he was short-handed, she knew that Eduardo wanted her back as soon as possible, and she had that freight run to make at one. She'd promised to pick up supplies for Jonathan Webber.

This might be cutting it close. "I can come back later if that's convenient—" Ellie began.

Debi was quick to interrupt her. "Dr. Dan really wants to talk to you."

Always accommodating, Ellie nodded. "All right, then I guess I can stay for a few minutes," she conceded. Looking around, she found an empty seat in the waiting area and sat beside Emma Hutchinson, a retired schoolteacher.

"You know," Emma confided to her new seatmate as if they were in the middle of a conversation, "for a sleepy little town, this place has got more commotion going on lately than a bustling metropolis."

Ellie did her best to hide the smile that statement generated. By no stretch of the imagination could Forever, Texas, be described as bustling—at least not in the present century. But Ellie saw no reason to antagonize the grandmother of four by pointing that simple fact out.

Instead she nodded. "I guess it seems that way some days. Especially if you're sitting in the middle of the medical clinic," she added, looking up at Debi. Only halfway into the morning and the head nurse already looked as if she was on the verge of being worn out.

Apparently, Debi had overheard the comment. "You can say that again," she murmured. The sound of an examination room door opening behind her had the nurse looking to her left. "The doctor'll see you now, Ellie." She promptly added, "Exam room three."

Rising, Ellie hurried around the wide reception desk and to the rear of the clinic.

The door to exam room three was standing open and Dan was just coming out to meet her when Ellie reached the hallway.

"Hello, Ellie," Dan greeted the young pilot. "Thanks for coming in so quickly." He stood back so that Ellie could enter. "Why don't you come in and take a seat?" he suggested.

Ellie crossed the threshold, still not sure just

what to think about the unexpected invitation. "Should I be worried?"

The question caught him by surprise. "What? No, why would you ask that?"

Ellie could see no reason why the doctor would ask her to come in—except for one. "Well, I was just here for my annual exam and you gave me a clean bill of health, but maybe there's something that you took a second look at and realized—"

"You're fine," Dan assured her quickly, not wanting her to labor under the wrong impression. "As it turns out," he said, getting right to the point, "I need your help. Specifically, I need to hire you to make a pickup."

The look of relief on her face was instantaneous. She was so busy trying to build up her business and also trying to help her grandfather, she didn't have time to deal with any health issues.

"Supplies or medications?" Ellie asked since the bulk of her flights had to do with transporting freight.

"Neither," Dan told her. "You'll be picking up and flying in a person."

"Oh?"

Rather than satisfy her curiosity, it just managed to raise it. She had never known the doctor—or his wife, for that matter—to have anyone come out for a visit. First time for everything.

Dan could see that Ellie was dying to ask questions. "Let me start at the beginning," he told her. "I'm sure you've heard about Miss Joan and the chest pains she's been having." He knew for a fact that after that first time at the diner, it had become the main topic of conversation whenever the woman was out of earshot. Everyone was concerned.

Never one to take stock of gossip, Ellie was still aware of it. She nodded. "Miss Joan should really listen to you. She's not a kid anymore and she shouldn't just play fast and loose with her health like that."

Dan laughed softly. "The rest of the town agrees with you, but that's not why I'm asking for your help."

Ellie put two and two together. "Let me guess. You want to kidnap Miss Joan and have me fly her to the hospital in Houston so she can be seen by a specialist." She rolled the idea over as she said it and nodded. "I'm your woman."

He laughed out loud at the scenario, although he wasn't surprised that it had crossed the young pilot's mind. "Well, I'm glad you're on board, but, as it turns out, a cardiologist friend of mine agreed to come out here to exam Miss Joan. He's flying in from New York City tomorrow."

Ellie took the information in stride. Now that she thought about it, she was not surprised that the doctor had that kind of pull. "Does Miss Joan know?"

Dan smiled. He was not looking forward to that confrontation, but he was hoping the woman would be reasonable once Neil arrived. "She will."

"So...no," Ellie concluded. This should be good, she thought. "Should I be getting ready to hold Miss Joan down once this doctor walks into her diner?"

"No," Dan laughed. "That's not why I need your services. Like I said, my friend will be flying in to Houston," he told her. "I need you to pick him up at the airport and fly him to Forever."

That sounded simple enough. "I'd be more than happy to," she told him. "But if you don't mind my asking, why isn't your friend renting a car and driving here?" she asked. "That would probably be simpler and that's what most people would do when they make a cross-country trip."

"The problem is Neil doesn't drive," Dan told her.

That really surprised her. Ellie could remember hounding her grandfather to teach her how to drive from the moment she could get behind the steering wheel and reach a gas pedal—with a little help. She had borrowed her late father's boots so that when she stretched, she could press down the pedal. Learning how to drive hadn't been just a rite of passage, it had been a symbol of independence.

"You're kidding," she said. "How has your friend been getting around up until now?"

"He lives in New York. Always has," Dan told her. "The city's blessed with a hell of a lot of public transportation and Neil never found the need or desire to learn how to drive anything except a hard bargain," he quipped. "Anyway, I'm getting sidetracked and I can tell from the sound of her voice that Mrs. Hutchinson is getting anxious," he said, referring to the patient he could hear voicing her impatience in the waiting room. "Can you pick up my friend?" he asked Ellie. "He's arriving at the Houston airport tomorrow. Are you free?"

"For you, Dr. Dan?" Ellie asked with a smile. "Always. I'll need all the particulars—his time of arrival and his flight number. Oh—" she'd thought of something else "—if you have a recent picture of the man, that'll be useful."

Nodding, Dan had already gotten all that. He reached into his lab coat pocket for the information. "He's flying out of JFK tomorrow morning at nine—New York time," he told her, producing the flight number. "And this is fairly recent photo of Neil." Dan held up his cell phone.

Ellie looked at the image on the doctor's phone. That was one good-looking man, she couldn't help thinking.

"Is he bringing his wife?" she asked. Because if he was, that would mean she'd need to prepare two seats on her plane.

Dan thought of the breakup Neil had told him about. "No, Neil's not married."

"Really?" she asked, taking a second look at the picture on the doctor's phone.

He decided to share the information with Ellie. At this point, he didn't think Neil would mind.

"He was engaged for a while, but that seems to be a thing of the past. I'm just lucky he's willing to come out here because Miss Joan really does need to be seen by a specialist. No one seems able to budge her or talk sense into her. Lord knows we've all tried. Harry and his grandson are really worried about her."

Dan shook his head as he approached the exam room door. "She didn't even want to come to see me," he confessed. "Cash threatened to carry her here if she didn't come in on her own power. I'm sure she only agreed to see my friend because Miss

Joan is certain he wouldn't come all this way to make a house call."

"House call?" Ellie repeated, slightly confused by the term.

"That's what they used to call it back in the old days. Before my time," he added in case Ellie was wondering just how old the term was.

She begged to differ with the doctor. "Oh, I don't know about that. When Pop had that appendicitis attack, you came out to see him in the middle of the night."

He remembered. He'd only been in town less than six months. Dan shrugged. "It's a small town. I can't afford to lose any patients."

She wasn't buying the excuse. In her opinion, when they'd made Dr. Dan, they'd broken the mold.

"Well, if you ask me, the town's lucky to have you—and there's no way we're ready to willingly lose Miss Joan." She followed Dan to the door. "I'll be at the Houston airport early," she promised. "And with any luck, I'll give your friend Neil the smoothest ride of his life getting him here." She paused just before leaving. "And if you have any trouble getting Miss Joan in to see your friend," she added, "I'm sure Pop, Addie and I would be more than happy to lend you a hand getting her out of the diner and into the clinic," she told him with a wink.

Dan smiled at the young woman. "I'll keep that in mind," he told her. "Let me know what the charge is."

"Just pay me for the fuel and we'll call it even," she said. "After all, I want to do my part keeping Miss Joan going."

They all did, Dan thought as Ellie left.

"Debi, send in Mrs. Hutchinson. I'm ready for her," he called out just before he went back into the exam room.

## *Chapter Four*

Eduardo made his way to the front door from the rear of the house just as Ellie was about to leave.

"I'm glad that I caught you before you left," he told his granddaughter.

Stopping in her tracks, Ellie curbed the urge to ask her grandfather if whatever this was could wait. She knew that Eduardo wasn't the type to run off at the mouth just to hear himself talk. The man was aware that she was in a hurry to get in the air, so it had to be important.

Biting back her impatience, she turned around to face the distinguished-looking rancher. "Just barely, Pop. What do you need?" she asked, one hand on the doorknob.

"Here, I made this for you," Eduardo told her. He passed Ellie a large placard. Written across it in big, bold, black letters was Dr. Neil Eastwood, the name of the doctor she was to pick up at the Houston air terminal.

Ellie looked at the sign a little uncertainly. "Um, it's very nice, Pop."

Eduardo could tell, by the way his granddaughter thanked him, that she was entirely in the dark about the placard's function. With a laugh, he proceeded to enlighten her.

"This way, if you hold this up in front of the people getting off the New York flight, the doctor who's coming in to see Miss Joan can find you instead of you having to spend a lot of time looking for him." He nodded at the sign. "Something else that used to be done back in the 'old' days," he told her.

"You made this?" Ellie asked, looking the placard over.

"Don't look so surprised. Raising horses and granddaughters isn't the only thing I do," Eduardo told her.

"A man of endless talents," she marveled with a smile. "Thank you, Pop." Ellie brushed a kiss against the man's gaunt cheek. "I appreciate this. It was very thoughtful of you."

The rancher waved away Ellie's words. "I just want you back sooner than later, that's all. Now, take off—literally," he ordered, shooing his grand-daughter on her way. "And don't forget to have a safe flight. Both ways," Eduardo added. Saying that was a superstition of his, and even though he knew wishing her a safe flight didn't guarantee she would have one, he didn't want to take any chances—just in case.

"Always." She smiled at him. "And thanks again for the sign," she said just before she dashed off to her makeshift airplane hanger to get into her aircraft.

The man really did think of everything, Ellie couldn't help thinking as she made her way through the air terminal to where the New York passengers would be disembarking in another few minutes.

The placard she was carrying felt a little cumbersome, but she didn't want to risk folding it. This way, if it wasn't creased, she felt the sign would be clearly visible when she held it up.

Ignoring the looks several people gave her as she sashayed around, trying to avoid hitting them with the edge of the placard, she found a spot near the front of a group of people. Everyone appeared to be waiting for the disembarking passengers to emerge.

Edging over to the middle, Ellie hoped that the sign would be clearly visible to everyone coming off flight number 324.

The sign was a really good idea, she thought again. She was only five foot four and that didn't always make it easy for her to see people. Ellie picked up the placard and held it above her head. With any luck, the doctor would be one of the first passengers off the plane. If he wasn't, she wasn't all that sure just how long she could hold the sign up before her arms became really tired.

She would have to start working her arms a little more, Ellie thought as an ache began to set in in her forearms. Taking a breath, she braced herself and continued holding the sign up above her head.

*Any minute now*, she promised herself, doing her best to scan the faces of the passengers emerging out of the passageway.

The flight appeared to be a full one. The disembarking passengers just kept coming, without giving any indication that the flood of people would stop any time soon.

Ellie began to regret not having asked her sister to come with her. Two sets of eyes were better than one and Addie was always looking for ways to get out of working on the ranch. This time it would have been for a good cause, Ellie mused. And more than that, they could have taken turns holding up the sign, which felt as if it was getting very, very heavy.

Several very long minutes later, Ellie began to entertain the idea that maybe this Dr. Eastwood had missed his flight. If he had, that would mean she would have to hang around the Houston airport until later today, or even that she'd possibly have to come back here tomorrow.

Her arms were really aching now. Ellie put down the sign and scanned the handful of passengers still trickling off the New York flight. Just about ready to give up hope, she heard a deep voice from behind her say, "I'm Dr. Neil Eastwood. Are you looking for me?"

Startled and still clutching the sign, although no longer holding it up, Ellie swung around to look at the person who had just spoken to her. She all but smacked the man in the chest with the sign bearing his name.

He stepped back out of the way to avoid the collision just at the last minute, but she still thought that she had hit him.

"Oh, I'm so sorry," Ellie cried, dropping the sign. "Did I hit you?" she asked, embarrassed.

"No, you didn't," Neil assured her. "Would you like to try again?" he deadpanned.

"No. No, of course not," she answered more seriously. "It's just that you startled me," she explained, struggling not to turn red. "I was watching for you, but I guess you must have gotten by me. Good thing Pop made this sign."

Ellie realized that she was babbling, something she had a tendency to do when she was caught at a disadvantage. Now that the doctor had arrived, she folded the placard to make it easier to carry. Tucking it under her arm, she extended her hand to the tall, blond-haired man towering over her.

"I'm sorry for the confusion," she apologized. "I'm Ellie Montenegro. Dr. Davenport sent me to give you a ride to Forever." Somehow, that just didn't sound right to her ear, like something was missing. "That's our town," Ellie tacked on, which still only seemed to make things worse.

The next second, she pressed her lips together. She stopped talking altogether for a moment and took in a deep, cleansing breath.

And then she tried again. "Dr. Dan is going to be very happy to see you. On behalf of Dr. Dan, as well as the rest of our town, I'd like to thank you for doing this—for coming out to Forever to give Miss Joan that much needed heart exam. We would—all of us—" she emphasized, "be very lost without that woman and her glib tongue passing judgment on us."

Amused, Neil inclined his head as if there really was no need to thank him for doing any of this. After all, he was a doctor. This was what he did. Besides, it was fulfilling some inner need of his.

"I'm way overdue for a vacation and I have to admit that Dan made this town sound very inter-esting." Another word would have been "quirky" but he decided to keep that to himself.

When the woman sent to meet him looked as if she was at a loss for a response, Neil decided that perhaps she needed to be prodded a little. So he did. "Shall we get going?" Neil suggested.

Ellie immediately snapped to attention, embar-rassed that she had somehow managed to drop the ball because she was mesmerized by his good looks.

"Yes, of course. I'm sorry, this just threw me off a little. You're actually my first airport pickup," she confessed.

Whenever she flew anyone anywhere, it usually involved dropping them off at a secluded cabin or some other inaccessible place in Texas. She didn't do airport runs. Not until now.

Ellie smiled to herself. Business was expanding.

"Well, then I guess I'm honored," Neil told her. "Speaking of firsts," he said as he started to pick up the carry-on luggage he had temporarily set down, "this is my first 'errand of mercy' flight."

Only half listening, Ellie had put her hand over the suitcase handle, intending to pick it up. When he looked at her in surprise, she told him, "Oh, I can take that for you." She deliberately moved his hands away and caught herself thinking that his hands felt as if they were very large and capable. How was he able to do delicate surgery with those hands? she wondered.

"I can carry my own suitcase," Neil told her, making a move to secure the handle.

But Ellie stubbornly kept her hand where it was, not allowing him take the case from her.

"Dr. Dan said you're a surgeon," she told him. "You don't want to risk hurting your hands."

"It's a suitcase," Neil pointed out. "Not a machete or an anvil. I can certainly carry a suitcase to your car."

"Actually," she corrected him, "We're taking it to my plane."

A plane? That surprised him. Dan had told him

that he was making arrangements to transport him from the airport to Forever. But his friend had said nothing about the arrangements involving a passenger plane. Or, for that matter, a sexy pilot.

"You have a plane?" Neil asked.

Leading the way out of the airport, Ellie happily nodded.

"It's a 2006 single-engine-turbine Piper Meridian." Seeing that meant nothing to him, she quickly added, "It doesn't look like much. But it's very safe."

"A Piper Meridian," Neil repeated. He had never heard of the plane before—at least, he thought she was talking about a plane. Maybe it wasn't safe to make any assumptions. "Is that the name of your airline?"

"No, that's the name of the type of plane I'm flying." Since, in a manner of speaking, he was entrusting her with his life, Ellie felt she owed him a little more of an explanation. "I'm hoping to someday have my own airline. Right now, there's just the one plane."

"Everyone has to start somewhere," he said philosophically. "And this aircraft…it's yours?" he asked, trying to get a handle on the woman he was apparently entrusting with his life.

Her smile was broad as she flashed it at him over her shoulder. "Technically."

That didn't sound all that good. "Technically?" he asked as they went through the airport's electronic doors to the outer area.

"Well, I'm still paying it off," she confided. "I bought the plane from Arnie. He was the one who owned the airline, but he decided to retire early last year. He sold all his planes but the one to another airline. I managed to talk him into selling that one plane to me." She glanced to the doctor. "I guess you probably think that's kind of unusual."

"I've never met anyone with their own aircraft before," he told her, trying to word his response as diplomatically as possible.

Her full lips pulled back into a quick smile. "Well, I've never met a heart surgeon before, so I guess that makes us even," Ellie said.

They crossed to what was a designated airfield reserved for private planes. Ellie gestured over to the side where she had left her aircraft before entering the terminal. The plane looked a little forlorn amid the other handful of planes that had been left there, awaiting their owners.

All the other planes appeared to be a lot newer than hers was. It didn't matter to her. She loved that old aircraft. Ellie waved her passenger over to the Piper Meridian.

"Lucille's right over there," she told him, picking up her pace.

"Lucille?" Neil questioned.

"The plane," Ellie clarified, gestured at the aircraft again.

But Neil was still having trouble assimilating the information. "You named your plane Lucille?" he asked, thinking Dan had obviously failed to mention how unusually colorful these people who lived in Forever were.

"No, I didn't," she told the doctor, which only seemed to further confuse the man. She spoke quickly to rectify that—or to attempt to at any rate. "Arnie was the one who called the aircraft Lucille. I just decided to leave it that way rather than confuse things further by changing her name."

"Afraid you'd confuse the plane if you called it by another name?" Neil asked, doing his best to try to follow the thread of the conversation. She didn't exactly make it easy. Nonetheless, he was amused.

"No, me," she said. When he looked at her curiously, she explained, "I just got used to calling the plane Lucille." They had reached the aircraft and she'd stopped walking.

"Sorry, I didn't mean to make it sound as if I

was making fun of you," he apologized in case that was what she thought he was doing. "Actually, one of the surgeons I work with has a Ferrari he calls 'Big Red.'"

Ellie opened the plane's door and released its stairway. She made no comment about the Ferrari. To her that vehicle was a sinful waste of money, but everyone was entitled to do whatever they wanted with their money—even waste it.

"Go on up," she told the doctor, gesturing toward the opened hatch. Neil looked a little skeptical about the venture. "Lucille doesn't bite," she assured him with a smile.

"I'll hold you to that," he told her before he gamely climbed up the steps that led into the plane. The stairs felt somewhat rickety to him, but he told himself that Dan wouldn't have made these arrangements for him if this method of travel wasn't at least safe.

Dan had sounded rather eager to have him come out to examine this friend of his, so Neil felt it was a pretty safe bet that he wouldn't be risking his life on this venture.

Still, he had to admit that he held his breath with every step he took to reach the inside of the aircraft.

Once he was seated, he heard his "pilot" call up to him, "Don't forget to put your seat belt on."

Taking a breath and thinking he had done smarter things in his life, Neil did as she had instructed. The moment he did, his diminutive pilot, moving agilely, climbed into the plane.

The door slamming shut sounded almost ominous to Neil, like the echo of a death knell. Turning toward Ellie, he asked, "And you *do* know how to fly this thing?"

A whimsical smile played on her lips. "Well, I'd better, don't you think?" she asked him. He looked at her with widened eyes. "I'm just kidding," Ellie assured him with a laugh. "Don't worry, I've logged in a lot of hours flying Lucille. I even have a license and everything," she teased, catching her tongue between her teeth. "And if it makes you feel any better, Dr. Dan cleared me for another year."

"Cleared you?" Neil repeated, obviously confused by the term.

"He said I was fit to fly a plane for another year." Going through her check list mentally, Ellie paused to look at her passenger. "Flying so high above the rest of the world is a wonderful experience, Doctor. There's really nothing that even comes close. You feel like you're one with the universe," she told him.

That revelation didn't exactly fill him with a great deal of confidence. "As long as you *don't* become one with the universe," he told her, thinking that a plane crash could easily accomplish that.

Ellie read between the lines. She needed to make him comfortable about this experience. "Well, I thought you'd want to get to Forever quickly and this is a lot faster than driving," Ellie told the surgeon. "Quite honestly, more people die in car crashes than in plane crashes."

"All it takes is once," he murmured.

"Don't worry," she assured him as the plane revved up. "I'll get you there safe and sound."

But Neil hardly seemed to hear her. At the moment, the surgeon was too busy clutched to his armrests and white-knuckling it.

## Chapter Five

If she didn't know any better, Ellie would have said that the muscular, good-looking man in the seat beside her was afraid of flying. In her estimation, he looked almost frozen in place. Maybe he was just uncomfortable. There could be any one of a number of reasons for that. In that case, she decided, it was her job to make him feel more comfortable.

"I take it you don't like to fly very much," Ellie said to him. She raised her voice to be heard above the noise generated within the passenger plane that, unfortunately, was rattling like a blender filled to the brim with cupfuls of loose screws.

It took Neil a second to realize that she was talking to him and then several more to actually make out the words she was saying. He found the noise level in the plane pretty bad.

"Not in a plane that sounds as if it is going to come apart at the seams any second now," he answered. "Are you *sure* this plane is going to make it?" Neil asked, because it certainly didn't sound that way to him.

"Oh, I'm sure," Ellie assured him. "I've flown this little gem when it sounded a lot worse than this," Ellie added.

"Why?" he asked.

For the life of him, he couldn't see taking a chance on flying something that, in his estimation, would have been upgraded in status if it was referred to as a "bucket of bolts."

Ellie shrugged. She assumed that he was asking her why she loved to fly. When it came right down to it, she really couldn't explain why, she just did.

"I guess I just love the freedom of soaring through the sky," she told the doctor. "It's in my blood." Her face brightened as she looked straight ahead through the windshield. "We're almost there," she told Neil, pointing. "If you concentrate really hard, you can almost *see* Forever right there in front of you."

"Forever," Neil murmured, focusing on the word as if it was a prediction. "Yeah, that's what I'm worried about."

"The town," she clarified with a laugh. "Not eternity." He might as well prepare himself, she thought. "Now, I should warn you—"

Neil was instantly on the alert. "Warn me?" he echoed, feeling nerves sprouting in his system. "About what?"

"The weather's a little turbulent right now..." she pointed out, although that was probably unnecessary, given how the surgeon was watching everything intently. "So the landing might be a bit bumpy—"

"But we are going to land, right?" Neil asked, interrupting her.

Ellie spared him a wide grin. "Yes, we are going to land," she assured the doctor, then added, "You might find it reassuring to know that I haven't crashed even once yet."

"All it takes is once," she heard him mutter under his breath.

Her smile grew wider, hoping that would reassure him. To look at the surgeon, Neil Eastwood didn't really appear nervous. But then, looks could easily be deceiving.

"Today is *not* a good day to die," Ellie told him,

putting a spin on an old Native American saying. "So we're just not going to."

He slanted a glance in her direction. It did *not* reflect the soul of confidence.

"You can't guarantee that," Neil pointed out. He grabbed onto the armrests, clutching them even harder as the rickety plane encountered even more turbulence.

Ellie was attempting to compensate for the rough weather, and the winds that had kicked up, by remembering everything she had been taught to keep the aircraft steady.

"Tell you what," she said gamely. "If we crash, I'll return your airfare."

Neil glared in the woman's direction before turning to face front again. He was hardly breathing as he did his best to will the plane to keep aloft.

"I didn't pay any airfare," he reminded her through gritted teeth.

"Well, then I guess I have nothing to worry about," Ellie quipped. "Relax, Dr. Eastwood. I've never lost a passenger yet."

"That doesn't really fill me with that much confidence," he told her. His hands were growing even whiter as he held on to the armrests.

Maybe he should have taken a sedative, she thought. Right now his behavior was making them both tense. And then she breathed a sigh of relief for both of them. The flight was almost over.

"There's Forever," Ellie pointed to the town that lay straight ahead of them. She smiled encouragingly at her passenger, secretly thinking that transporting animals was a great deal easier than bringing in Dr. Dan's friend. "We're coming in for a landing," she announced and then smiled at him. "I can hold your hand if that would make you feel any better."

"You landing this plane in one piece will make me feel a whole lot better," Neil told her, staring at the swiftly approaching ground as they were about to land.

Ellie nodded. "Your wish is my command, Doc."

Mentally, she went through the checklist for a proper, uneventful landing, the way she always did. She did it each and every time she landed even though she knew all the steps by heart.

"Okay, Doc, here we go," Ellie announced, telling him to, "Brace yourself."

"If I were any more braced," Neil answered, "I'd snap in half."

"No, no snapping in half on my watch," Ellie deadpanned. She knew he was kidding. At least, she *hoped* he was. "There's an extra charge for that."

Neil glanced at her. How could the woman make jokes at a time like this? In the few moments that the plane had begun its descent, his stomach had lurched upward and now felt as if it was firmly lodged in his mouth, threatening to gag him.

Neil's entire body was tensed and braced, waiting to feel what promised to be a really jarring impact as the plane prepared to touch down on what looked like the world's shortest runway.

When it finally did land, Neil wasn't sure whether to utter a cry of joy or just shed a few tears of immense gratitude and relief.

The surgeon settled for offering up a few heartfelt, albeit silent, words of thanksgiving. The ordeal was finally over!

With the plane back on Mother Earth, Ellie slowly brought it to a halt then turned off all the plane's switches one by one. When she had flipped the last one, she turned toward her passenger. It was all too obvious that the doctor had definitely *not* enjoyed the ride.

Ellie did her best not to smile. "You can let go of the armrests, Doc. We've landed."

She heard Neil release a shaky breath. Ellie realized that she hadn't heard him breathing during the last part of the landing. Had he really been that afraid?

And then she heard him say, "I guess prayers do get answered," and she had her answer.

"Well, you're proof of that," she responded glibly. Neil looked at her as if he didn't understand, so she did her best to explain. "You're the mountain who came to Mohammed. In this case, Miss Joan was playing the part of Mohammed. Everyone in town knew we didn't have a prayer of getting her to see a doctor anywhere outside of Forever. Just when it all seemed so hopeless, you agreed to fly in and see her."

Neil found he was still trying to release his death grip on the armrests and relax his hands. "I wouldn't have agreed if I had known everything that was involved."

For the moment, Ellie remained sitting in the plane—not because *she* needed to but because she wanted Neil to be able to navigate off the airplane— she didn't want him to suffer the embarrassment of his knees buckling. She'd witnessed it before and she wanted to spare him that.

"Then I guess it's lucky for us you didn't know what was involved—although it wouldn't have been nearly so complicated for you if you had only known how to drive," she diplomatically pointed out.

Neil opened his mouth to argue that point but knew that, in all fairness, he really couldn't. At bottom, he supposed he had to admit that it was his own fault he'd had to face the harrowing flight through the heavens.

"Learning how to drive just went to the top of my to-do list," he assured the pilot.

"I could teach you," Ellie offered cheerfully. "I've been driving ever since I was eleven years old."

Somehow, he didn't doubt it. "Do you drive like you fly?" he asked, even though he wasn't really considering her offer.

Ellie grinned at him. "There's less turbulence on the ground than there is in the air—at least today—so I'd probably have to say 'better.' Think about it."

"Right now," he told her very honestly, "all I want to do is just feel the earth under my feet."

"Hold on," Ellie instructed.

The next thing Neil knew, she had opened the door on her side and, rather than take the stairs, had jumped to the ground as agilely as his Great-Aunt Grace's cat used to when the calico would spring off the kitchen windowsill in the dead of winter.

Craning his neck to catch sight of his pilot as

she disappeared from view, Neil called out to her. "Hello? Ellie?"

Had she suddenly decided to abandon him?

Just as the question flashed through his mind, Neil thought he heard a noise coming from outside the passenger window. Turning his head, he caught a glimpse of jet-black hair flying by. The next thing he knew, the door on his side had opened.

Ellie was on the ground, releasing the door and the steps on that side. She beckoned to him. "C'mon down," she invited.

Neil took a deep breath, focusing on his feet finally being able to touch the ground. Just before he attempted to climb out, he frowned. Why did climbing down look so much more intimidating than climbing up had?

While he supposed that he was as agile as the next person, he really wasn't exactly the last word in gracefulness. He had always been the kind of man who usually looked before he leaped. Right now, looking had a way of interfering with the perfect execution of what he was attempting to do.

Like getting out of a plane without twisting his ankle.

Still, not wanting to fall on his face in front of a ravishing brunette was a definite motivator. Neil braced himself and quickly climbed down, listening to the rickety steps issue their own protest.

And then he was finally on the ground.

No one was more relieved than Ellie was, although she kept that to herself.

"Okay," she said breezily, climbing back up into the plane and retrieving the doctor's suitcase for him. Moving swiftly back out, she put it next to him on the ground. "The rest is easy now."

"Oh?" Neil didn't know whether he should brace himself again or believe her and breathe a sigh of relief.

"Yes. I'm going to drive you into town now to see Dr. Dan."

Ellie led the way over to where she had parked her Jeep this morning. It was still in the field, waiting for her, the way she knew that it would be. She had anticipated having to drive the doctor into town and to the medical clinic once she had flown him in.

Neil examined the vehicle. It was clean, looked as if it had not only some miles on it but some years, as well.

He asked her the same question he had earlier, waiting for an honest answer. "Do you drive as well as you fly?"

Ellie inclined her head. "Almost as well," she answered, tongue in cheek.

"Should I be praying?"

"Only if you want to," Ellie answered glibly. And then she couldn't help herself. She laughed as she threw his suitcase into the back and then climbed in on the driver's side. "I thought all of you New Yorkers were supposed to be fearless."

"We are, but there is a definite difference between fearless and foolhardy. I'm trying to decide which you represent." Neil paused, his eyes washing over her face and accessing what he saw. "I haven't made up my mind yet."

His answer made her grin, not to mention created a tingle that fanned out into every part of her. "I'll take that as a compliment."

"I'm not sure if I meant it that way," he admitted, "but okay. Whatever works for you."

Getting into the Jeep, he buckled up and then looked at his driver. He realized that she was observing him and there was a wide, amused smile on her lips.

"What?" he asked, braced for a flippant answer.

"I think this is going to be a really interesting adventure for you during the next few days," Ellie told him.

His eyes met hers and, for the first time since

it had happened, he was really glad that he and Judith had broken up. "I think it already is," he agreed.

"Glad to hear it," Ellie told him, starting up the Jeep. "Okay, let's go show Dr. Dan that I brought you in safe and sound."

"Well, at least you brought me in," Neil replied, not altogether certain yet about the "safe and sound" part of her statement.

Hearing him, Ellie laughed, and he found himself really liking the sound of her laughter. Unbidden, something warm stirred within him.

Heads turned, the way they always did, when the medical clinic's front door opened. With little to do but read outdated magazines, the patients sitting in the waiting room eagerly looked upon any diversion as a welcome distraction from the tediousness of watching for the minute hand move slowly around the face of the clock.

So whenever anyone new entered into the clinic, all eyes automatically turned toward the newcomer or newcomers.

Ellie Montenegro was a familiar sight in Forever, but the tall blond man walking next to her was definitely not. Several of the female patients in the room sat a little straighter. A few consciously pulled in their stomachs and others just stared un-abashedly, memorizing the handsome stranger's every feature—and could, at the very least, recre-ate his face on paper if anyone were to ask.

Unless Ellie missed her guess, a bevy of ques-tions seemed to be materializing in their heads.

"If you'll just sign in, please," Debi said, ad-dressing the newcomer next to Ellie with a warm, inviting smile.

"Oh, he's not a patient, Debi," Ellie told the nurse before Neil even got the chance. "Dr. Dan is waiting to see him. He's the cardiac specialist the doctor sent me to pick up from the Houston airport."

The moment Ellie told her that, Debi was in-stantly on her feet.

"Wait right here," Debi told the duo as she quickly went to the back of the clinic.

Dan was in exam room 2 and she knocked on the door twice in quick succession. "Dr. Dan, Ellie is here and she brought that package you've been waiting for."

The door opened almost immediately. "Where is he?" Dan asked, looking over Debi's shoulder as if half expecting his friend to be standing right there. It had been a long time since they had seen one another and, along with wanting Neil to exam Miss Joan, he was also eager to see the man.

"He's in the waiting room right now, along with Ellie," Debi replied.

Dan nodded, pleased that his friend had arrived safely. "Tell him to take a seat and I'll be right out to get him as soon as I finish examining Miss Albright," he told his nurse.

Nodding, Debi promised, "I'll let him know." Making her way back to her desk in the waiting area, she approached the specialist as well as Ellie, who was still waiting there with the doctor. "Dr. Dan said for you to take a seat. He'll be right out to see you as soon as he finishes examining Miss Albright," she told Dr. Dan's friend. "You can sit right over here," she prompted, pointing out two recently vacated seats. "It won't take long. He was just finishing up."

"Thank you," Neil said.

He made his way over to the seats and proceeded to make himself comfortable, trying not to notice that everyone seemed to be staring at him.

At least he was safely on the ground, he thought, trying to take solace in that.

## Chapter Six

"Well," Ellie said as she rose even though she had just taken her seat, "I've got to be getting back to the ranch." She was happy to see that Neil's color had completely returned and he no longer appeared to be the worse for his experience.

Neil rose to his feet, as well. "You have a ranch?" he asked. He assumed that her claim to fame was flying freight, and occasionally people, in that little plane of hers—which he had found unusual enough. Apparently, people in Western towns wore a great many hats, Neil thought.

"My grandfather owns the ranch. My sister, Addie, and I live on it and do what we can to help him out," Ellie explained, supplying a thimbleful of background information. She paused, her hand on the doorknob. "If you should need anything else, Doc, Dr. Dan knows where to find me."

"And if he's not available at the time, everyone else in town knows where to find her, too," Eva Whitman volunteered.

Several of the patients in the waiting room nodded their heads, assuring the specialist of that piece of information.

"Good to know," Neil replied cryptically. The cardiac surgeon had to admit that he wasn't exactly accustomed to living in an area where everyone's business was thought of as community property. He politely kept that to himself and nodded his head. Turning to the departing pilot, he said to Ellie, "Thanks again for the ride."

Ellie couldn't help but laugh in response. When the doctor raised a quizzical eyebrow, questioning her reaction, she told him, "You know you don't really mean that, but you're welcome."

He saw dimples in her cheeks and was totally charmed by them, but he had no idea how to respond to her statement—because she was right. The plane ride had come perilously close to making him recycle his last meal, but at the same time, the woman had been under no obligation to make the trip to Houston to pick him up.

Fortunately for him, Neil didn't have to say anything in response because, at that moment, Dan entered the waiting area.

"C'mon in, Neil," he said to his friend.

"Are you expanding your practice again, Dr. Dan?" Silas McCormick asked, raising his voice to be heard above the ongoing din. "It's been a while since you brought in anyone new, like that lady doctor who came here."

Joyce Vance, a widow for the last three years, was quick to attempt to convince the new doctor to put down his roots in Forever. "This is a really great, up-and-coming place to move to," she told Neil. "Am I right?" the woman asked, looking at her closet seatmate as if the answer was a foregone conclusion.

Dan saw the not-so-subtle plea for help written on his friend's face and came to his rescue. "Settle down, folks. Don't scare the man away before he even opens up his suitcase. Dr. Eastwood's only here to examine Miss Joan."

At the mention of Forever's venerable, beloved-if-cranky matriarch, the people in the waiting room became properly respectful.

"About time someone finally gave that woman a

much needed examination. She can't expect to just keep going the way she's been going and pressing her luck." Jonah Timberlane turned toward one of the women in the room. "I was there when she collapsed, you know," he said importantly.

*"Almost collapsed,"* Vic Allen corrected, clearing his throat. "Miss Joan never hit the ground," the retired miner pointed out.

This had all the makings of the breakout of a prolonged argument. "Come into my office," Dan urged his friend, gesturing toward the rear of the clinic. "It's right this way."

"Nice meeting you, Dr. Eastwood," one of the women called out, raising her voice. "Hope you decide to stay here."

Pretending not to hear, Neil didn't answer. But the moment he and Dan left the reception area, he looked at the man ultimately responsible for convincing him to come here for a consultation.

"Are they *always* like that?" he asked Dan a little uneasily.

"No, they're usually a lot more vocal and in-your-business," he told Neil seriously.

Dan managed to keep a straight face for another thirty seconds then laughed. "Welcome to Forever," he told his friend, "where everyone doesn't just know your name, they know absolutely *every-*

*thing* about you, your family and about your second cousin, twice removed. Why don't you take a
seat?" Dan gestured to the chair facing his desk.

Neil sank down onto the chair, shaking his
head. "Wow, talk about being nosy."

"These people aren't nosy," Dan told the heart
surgeon. "They care. There is a difference."

Neil didn't appear to be all that convinced. "If
you say so."

"I do," Dan insisted. He had learned that fact
over the years. "That's why they were all so concerned about getting Miss Joan to see a specialist—
and why Ellie flew out to fetch you and wouldn't
take any money for doing it—outside of being re-
imbursed for the fuel."

"'Fetch' me?" Neil repeated, marveling at his
friend's wording. "Wow, you really *have* changed,"
he couldn't help observing and then pointing out,
"That wouldn't have fit into your vocabulary ten
years ago."

"A lot of things aren't what they used to be any
more," Dan told the other doctor. "And I have to
say that I kind of like the change."

"Seriously?" Neil asked, amazed.

"Seriously," Dan assured him. He didn't want
to seem as if he was being Spartan. "Oh, I might
occasionally miss having three hundred channels

to choose from, but to be very honest, what with my really heavy patient load, my beautiful wife and my very active kids, I don't really even have the time to go flipping through all those channels any more."

"How *is* your wife?" Neil asked.

"Getting more and more beautiful every day," Dan told his friend happily. In his opinion, she had really blossomed in the years they had been together. "You can see for yourself tonight."

"I'm looking forward to it," Neil told him. "And by the way, when do I finally get to meet this Miss Joan of yours?"

"Oh, she's not *my* Miss Joan," Dan assured Neil. "She's everyone's Miss Joan and, at the same time, she's her own person."

Neil laughed softly under his breath. "Sounds like she's quite a character."

Leaning back in his chair, Dan grinned with appreciation. "That's the word to describe her, all right," he agreed. Just then, there was a quick knock on his door. "Come in," he invited.

His other nurse opened the door and partially peered into the office. There was an apologetic look on the young woman's face.

"Dr. Dan, Ms. Whitman is getting a little rambunctious out there."

"Ms. Whitman?" Neil echoed. "Is that the white-haired woman I just met out in your office?"

Dan stood. It was time to get back to his patients. "One and the same," he assured his friend.

"'Rambunctious,' huh?" he repeated, amused. "Now *that* I'd really like to see," Neil admitted. The woman had looked extremely subdued. Apparently, Ms. Whitman was not.

Dan laughed. "Stick around long enough and I can practically guarantee it," he promised his friend as a thought occurred to him and he turned to his nurse. "Trudy, could you call my wife and have her come by so that Neil is able to get settled into the house while he's staying here?"

"Sure thing, Doctor," his nurse replied. "I'll get right on it."

"Dan, I don't need an escort," Neil protested. "Just tell me how to get there and I'll be out of your hair."

But Dan just shook his head. He remembered how disorienting everything out here had been for him at first. "You come from the city where half the streets are sequentially numbered. You don't appreciate that until that's not the case. Trust me, it'll be better if I have someone show you the way."

"Dr. Dan, why don't I ask Ellie to take your friend over to your house?" the nurse suggested.

"Ellie?" Dan questioned. He thought she'd left. "Is she still here?"

"Not 'still,'" the nurse corrected. "She came back, but she just left," Trudy told him. "It seems she forgot to pick up a prescription for her grandfather. I can still catch her for you if you want."

Dan nodded. That seemed to be the best way to proceed. "Please," he urged his nurse. "If you don't mind?"

"That's really not necessary, Dan." Neil was attempting to talk his friend out of doing this.

But Dan was not about to be talked out of it. "Yes," he insisted, "it is." Turning, he looked at his nurse. "Trudy?"

"I'm on it," the woman affirmed, hurrying out the door.

For his part, Neil looked far from happy about this turn of events as he walked out into the reception area.

By the time he had reached it, the woman who had taught him the true concept of "flying by the seat of her pants" had just reentered the clinic. Their eyes met and Ellie grinned at him.

"You know, Doc, we've got to stop meeting like this," she quipped.

"My thoughts exactly," Neil told her without the least bit of a hint of a smile to underscore his words.

"Ellie, Dr. Dan said he hoped you wouldn't mind doing him this one more favor…" Trudy began.

Ellie shook her head. "Not a bit," she assured the nurse.

Neil hated imposing and this felt like a huge imposition. "I thought you said that you had to get back to your grandfather," he reminded Ellie as they walked out the front door.

"Oh, I do," she replied. "But there's no emergency—and Pop will be happy to know that I'm late because of a good cause."

In an odd sort of way, her words rang a familiar bell for Neil. "My father would have never thought that being late for any reason was because of a good cause," Neil told her, thinking back to his childhood. His father had been a parent who had ruled with an iron fist—and refused to put up with anything.

"That's probably because your father didn't grow up in Forever," Ellie told him, leading the way back to her Jeep. "Out here, everyone multitasks."

There seemed to be something wrong with that, Neil couldn't help thinking. "Don't you people wind up burning out early?"

She rolled over his question in her mind. "Another way to look at it is that multitasking invigorates us and helps to inspire us," she told him. She pointed to a far corner of the clinic's parking area. "My Jeep's right there."

"I remember," he told her, his tone slightly dismissive because he couldn't shake the feeling that she was talking down to him.

"I just meant that I hadn't had a chance to move the Jeep yet. I remembered about my grandfather's prescription just when I got to the Jeep and did an about-face to go get it."

Neil realized that the woman was apologizing, when he was the one who owed her an apology.

"Sorry, I didn't mean to snap at you like that," he told her. "I suppose that I'm being a little testy right now."

Ellie didn't want him dwelling on the apology. To her, it was just a waste of energy. "You're entitled," the pilot told him. "This is all kind of new to you."

"It's not *that* new," he insisted. It's not as if he had never apologized for anything before. And then, thinking about his mindset back in New York, he lowered his defenses just a little. "I thought I wanted something new and different, but I'm beginning to realize that I'm not all that crazy about change, after all," he confessed.

Ellie understood perfectly. "Don't feel bad about it. Most people aren't," she told him. "At least, not to begin with. Change means having to give up the familiar, to give up something you're comfortable with. When that happens, there's a part of you that feels as if maybe you're making a mistake—until you find, to your surprise, that you like the change, after all."

That sounded pretty deep, he couldn't help thinking—and totally out of character for this part of the country. "What makes you such an expert on change?" he asked.

"Oh, I'm not," she told him. "I'm just speculating. I like to daydream that I'm going to all these exotic places, but I never have. Maybe that's the real reason why I like flying so much. It gives me the opportunity to pretend I'm going to all these different places but I actually never really have to take off anywhere." She flashed a smile at the doctor as she began to drive over to the Davenport house. "Does that make any sense to you?"

Neil's first reaction was to say "No," but then he gave her words some deeper consideration and wound up surprising himself.

"Oddly enough," he admitted, "it kind of does."

Maybe whatever the pilot had was catching. His brain felt as scrambled as her words had sounded, he couldn't help thinking.

Maybe something else was at fault. "Just how high is the altitude up here?"

She laughed. "Not high enough to play havoc with your brain, Doctor, I promise. You know," she continued, "it's nice that you're open-minded like this."

"Why's that?" he asked, curious to understand what she was going to come up with. He didn't expect actual logic.

"Because it'll help prepare you for dealing with Miss Joan—at least as much as anything could when to comes to the woman."

"You make her sound like some sort of a rare enigma," he said, then realized that he was probably talking over the pilot's head.

It surprised him that he wasn't. "Oh, she's that and much more," Ellie assured him. "A *lot* more."

He thought of all the characters he had encountered during his hospital residency in the ER in New York.

"She can't be that bad," he told Ellie.

"Trust me, she is," she assured him. "Miss Joan is…well… Talk to me *after* you've had a chance to meet her and tell her something that she *doesn't* want to hear."

"That sounds like a challenge," Neil told Ellie.

"Oh, it is," she agreed. "All that and more."

He couldn't really explain it, but for the first time in years, Neil suddenly caught himself looking forward to the encounter.

## Chapter Seven

The moment Addie saw Ellie land her plane and then taxi it into the renovated barn, she stopped doing what she was doing. Tossing aside her pitchfork, she ran to the barn so that by the time Ellie got out of her tiny Piper Meridian, Addie was right there inside the makeshift hanger, waiting for her older sister.

"So?" she asked expectantly the second that Ellie emerged.

Ellie dusted herself off. "So?" Ellie echoed quizzically. She had no idea just what her sister was asking her about.

"So what's this new doctor like?" Addie asked

impatiently. "Is he young? Is he cute? Is he easy to talk to? What *did* you two talk about? Do you think he's planning to stay in Forever? Dr. Dan wasn't planning on it when he came, but you know what happened there, so maybe this one—"

*Oh, Lord*, Ellie thought. Addie had a habit of drowning anyone close by in a sea of words. She held up her hands. "Breathe, Addie. Breathe!" she ordered her sister.

Addie pretended to go through the elaborate motion of drawing in a deep breath and then said, "Okay, so answer this for me—"

Ellie was busy getting her carryall out of the cockpit. Finding it, she slung the strap over her shoulder.

"Yes, he's cute. *Very cute*," she emphasized truthfully. "But I have no idea if he's planning on staying. I don't think he is—"

"But you could be wrong," Addie interjected. It was obvious to Ellie that, sight unseen, Addie had taken an interest in this supposed "new doctor in town" whether he actually was that or not.

"I could *always* be wrong," Ellie allowed.

Addie nodded as she walked out of the hanger with her sister and into the open space. "So what did he talk about?"

Recalling, Ellie smiled to herself. She'd had better conversations with strangers.

"Mainly, he wanted to know when we were going to land and did I think the landing was going to be a safe one," she told her sister. Slipping her hand into her pocket, her fingers brushed against the pills Dr. Dan's nurse had given her.

*Pop's prescription*, she thought. She wanted to get it to him before she forgot.

Ellie began walking fast toward the house.

Addie was still on the doctor's last conversation with her sister. "What did you do to him?"

"Nothing." Ellie tried not to take offense at Addie's insinuation. "The man obviously isn't used to planes that make loud, rattling noises when they fly," Ellie said with a shrug. "That was probably his first experience with a small passenger plane."

"Poor guy, maybe he needs to be comforted." Addie obviously felt she was just the one for the job. The boys in town who were around her age were all just that—boys. A young, well-to-do doctor was just what she needed to spice up her life. "Where did you say he was staying?" Addie asked, glancing in the direction of town. She gave every impression of being ready to rush right over there.

"What Neil Eastwood needs, Addie," Ellie told her sternly, "is to be left alone. He's going to be dealing with Miss Joan and that's more than enough for anyone to have on their plate at the moment."

But Addie saw it differently and wasn't about to let this opportunity slip through her fingers. "Maybe he needs to have someone offer him a hand when it comes to having to deal with Miss Joan," Addie suggested. "You know, I'm sure he'd be pretty grateful to someone who knew how to deal with Miss Joan—"

Ellie stopped walking and stared at her sister. "And what—that would be you?" she asked, surprised by what her sister was thinking. As far back as Ellie could remember, Addie had been intimidated by the tough-as-nails Miss Joan.

"Sure, why not?" Addie asked, tossing her head and sending her thick, straight black hair flying over her shoulder.

"'Why not?'" Ellie repeated incredulously. It took everything she had not to laugh at the image Addie was attempting to project. "Because the woman would eat you for breakfast and not even notice that she swallowed anything, that's why not."

"Oh, she's not an ogre," Addie insisted, waving her hand at the image Ellie was suggesting.

"No," Ellie agreed, "she's not. But Miss Joan

likes to make people keep their distance—unless she actually *wants* them to get closer."

Addie disregarded the point that Ellie was trying to make. "Maybe Neil would appreciate having a buffer," she said, refusing to give up on creating an "in" for herself with this new doctor.

Addie couldn't really be serious—could she? Ellie wondered. Where was this need to connect with a rich, handsome doctor coming from?

"He's a doctor, Addie," Ellie said, attempting to talk some sense into her sister. "I'm sure he deals with crabby, difficult people all the time. He won't need to have a buffer."

Addie looked at her, pity in her eyes. "Ellie, what happened to your heart?" she asked.

Okay, she'd been patient enough, Ellie thought. Time to stop trying to be diplomatic.

"Nothing happened to it. It's right where it's supposed to be. In my chest. As for you, you're just interested in meeting and cultivating an eligible doctor."

Addie didn't bother denying it. Instead, she raised her chin. "And if I was, what's wrong with that?"

"Nothing," Ellie told her. "If you're attracted to him and not to the *idea* of him. Besides, how do you know he's not married?"

The mere suggestion—something Addie hadn't even thought of—had her looking stricken. "Oh, El, he's not, is he?"

Ellie sighed and rolled her dark blue eyes. "No, Ad, he's not."

"How do you know?" Addie asked suspiciously. "Did he ask you out?" Were they going to be competing against each other? she suddenly wondered.

"No, Addie, he didn't ask me out," she told her sister. "When Dr. Dan made arrangements for me to pick up his friend at the airport, I asked Dr. Dan if his friend would be bringing his wife with him because, in that case, I'd need to clear an extra seat in the plane." She knew Addie would like this. "Dr. Dan said his friend had just recently broken up with his fiancée."

"Nice going," Addie said, impressed by the way Ellie had managed to get the information. She grinned, the dimples in her cheeks springing to life. "He just broke up, eh? The poor man needs comforting."

Ellie rolled her eyes. "Lord, Addie, doesn't your plane ever land?"

Addie stared at her sister. "You're the one with the plane, Ellie."

Ellie shook her head. She was wasting her time.

"Never mind. I've got to give Pop his pills," she said, holding up the medication.

Both sisters had always agreed that their grandfather's health was always their first priority.

"Okay, but don't forget that after that, you promised to help me pitch fresh hay in the stalls," Addie reminded her.

But Ellie had to bow out. "Sorry, Ad. I can't. I've got a couple of errands to run and then I have to get ready."

Perfectly arched dark eyebrows drew together as Addie gave her sister another questioning look. "Ready for what?"

"Dinner," Ellie replied innocently. "I've been invited out for dinner," she said, knowing that it wasn't going to die there.

"With who?"

"With 'whom,'" Ellie corrected.

"A grammar lesson?" Addie asked. "You're giving me a grammar lesson? Now? Seriously?"

"Seems appropriate," Ellie told her sister.

Addie's patience was swiftly evaporating. "An *answer* would be appropriate, El."

"I guess we'll just agree to disagree on that point, little sister," Ellie said cheerfully. "Now, if there's nothing else, let me go and give this to Pop so I can get on with my errands."

Addie made a sharp, guttural noise under her breath. Was Ellie attracted to the visiting surgeon or not? "Damn it, Ellie, you can be so very infuriating at times!"

Ellie flashed Addie a complacent smile as she passed by her sister. "Then I guess my work here is done," she said, her eyes sparkling with humor.

"C'mon, Ellie, who are you having dinner with?" Addie called after her, but Ellie managed to put a lot of distance between them very quickly as she headed toward the ranch house.

Walking in, Ellie found her grandfather in the kitchen, sitting at the table and nursing a cup of coffee that was swiftly disappearing.

Not his first, or his second, of the day, Ellie was willing to bet.

The man looked up when he heard his granddaughter enter.

"Did you find your doctor?" Eduardo asked.

"Not 'my doctor,' Pop," she corrected, thinking of Addie and how much her sister would have liked to have fielded that question. "But yes, thanks to that sign you made for me, I did. And here—" she dug into her front pocket and took out the prescription she had picked up for him "—I also got these for you." She handed the packet to her grandfather.

He frowned at the offering and didn't attempt to

take it from her. "I told Dr. Dan that I didn't have the money for that right now, Ellie."

He could be so stubborn, she thought. "You didn't pay for that, Pop."

"I'm not having you pay for it, either, Ellie," Eduardo insisted. How would it look to the men if he had her paying for things? Or to Ellie, for that matter?

"I'm not," Ellie assured her grandfather.

"Oh, so then you stole it," Eduardo said loftily.

She knew that the thought of accepting charity rankled her grandfather. He thought nothing of doling it out, but the man balked when it came down to accepting it.

"No. Dr. Dan said to think of it as a way of thanking me for going out of my way and bringing his friend to Forever to examine Miss Joan." She paused, looking at her grandfather. "Pop, you are the dearest person in the world to me—and to Addie," she added seriously. "And neither one of us is about to have your pride be responsible for putting your life in any sort of danger." She couldn't read her grandfather's expression. "And if that's being disrespectful, then I'm sorry, but there you have it. So please take your medication and stop giving me a hard time about it. I've got more than I can handle with Addie driving me crazy all the time," she told her grandfather. "Now, is there anything else?"

"No, not at the moment," Eduardo answered, the corners of his mouth curving affectionately. "You're a good girl, Ellie."

Ellie grinned at him. "You're just finding that out now, Pop?" she asked, pretending to ask the question seriously.

The gray-haired gentleman waved her off. "Go, do whatever it is you have to do. I'll have a couple of the boys pick up your slack. Oh, one last thing…" he said as another question occurred to him.

Ellie paused, waiting. "Go ahead."

"This specialist that Dr. Dan managed to get to come out," he began.

"What about him?" she asked, doubting her grandfather's questions were on the same level that Addie's had been. He, undoubtedly, had legitimate questions.

"Do you think he'll be able to get Miss Joan to listen to him, provided that what he has to tell her isn't something she would actually *want* to hear?" he asked, curious.

Eduardo wasn't saying anything that Ellie hadn't already wondered herself. Miss Joan wasn't exactly the easiest person to handle.

"Well, if he doesn't turn out to be forceful

enough to get her to agree to getting treatment—
and I think that there's probably a good chance that
he will have to—there's all the rest of us around
to gang up on the woman and *make* her listen to
reason." She paused then said, "At bottom, Miss
Joan is a reasonable person," Ellie insisted.

Eduardo smiled, nodding. "While that is true,"
her grandfather agreed, "there's something that
you have to understand."

Ellie wondered if this was something her grandfather was relating to himself and that she wasn't
going to want to hear.

"What?" she asked cautiously.

"As a person begins to grow older, fear has a
way of interfering with common sense. Maybe
Miss Joan is afraid to let those scary thoughts in
because, if she does, then they might just stand a
better chance of coming true." He looked at her,
trying to gauge her reaction to what he'd just said.
"Does that make any sense to you?"

"Too much, actually," Ellie admitted.

He smiled at his older granddaughter. "What
that means is that we're all going to have to be
there for her, like you said. Just the way that you
were for me." His eyes narrowed. "Don't think
I've forgotten what a bully you can be when you
want to be."

She put on an innocent expression. "I don't know what you're talking about," she told her grandfather with a laugh. And then she brushed a kiss on his cheek. "I'll see you later on tonight, Pop. And do me a favor, tell Addie that I'll make it up to her."

"Make what up to her?" Eduardo asked, curious what she was talking about.

She merely smiled at the man. Ellie didn't want to get into it because she was fairly sure that her sister wouldn't want their grandfather teasing her about the possible infatuation Addie might be harboring, sight unseen, for Dr. Dan's friend.

"She'll know," Ellie told her grandfather. "Now I'd better go before I wind up being late to the Davenport house for dinner."

Eduardo smiled to himself, pleased that his older granddaughter was actually taking a little time out for herself to socialize instead of just working around the clock. Heaven knew that Ellie deserved a little "me" time. She certainly was more than entitled to it, Eduardo thought.

Ellie had barely had enough time to take care of the handful of chores she had promised herself to do before she left the ranch house.

Avoiding Addie had been trickier, but some-how, Ellie'd managed to accomplish that, as well.

At the last minute, before she headed toward the Davenport house in town, Ellie swung by the Murphy brothers' saloon. She wanted to pick up a bottle of Pinot Grigio. Personally, Ellie didn't care for the taste of wine, but she knew that other people did. Even if the bottle wasn't opened at the table today, she was fairly confident that it would be put to good use somewhere down the line. She didn't feel right about showing up for dinner empty-handed.

Standing at the doctor's front door, she rang the doorbell. Several seconds went by and Ellie began to wonder if she had misunderstood the doctor's invitation and it had been for a different day. But then the door began to open.

She'd expected to see Dan or his wife on the other side of the entrance. Or, just possibly Dan's stepson, the little boy who had initially been the reason Dan's wife, Tina, had gone through Forever and why her older sister, the sheriff's wife, had come out here looking for Tina in the first place.

It occurred to Ellie that it had been a while since she had seen any of those people. She re-ally needed to find a little time to catch up, Ellie thought. Addie was right, she was much too busy

working at one thing or another to stop and enjoy
the company of old friends. That needed to stop,
Elli silently lectured herself as the front door finally opened.

It wasn't any member of the Davenport family who'd come to the door. Instead, the person
she was looking at across the threshold was Neil.

## *Chapter Eight*

It took Neil a second to process the fact that the woman who had flown him from the Houston airport—and was responsible for an unsettling amount of turmoil in the pit of his stomach, thanks to that flight—was standing right in front of him.

"Did we make arrangements to have me fly back to Houston?" he asked Ellie. "Because if we did, then it was premature. I haven't had a chance to meet and examine Miss Joan yet."

"Well, I can't say that I'm really surprised," Ellie told the specialist. "Miss Joan can play really hard to get when she wants to."

"What are you doing, standing outside, Ellie?"

Tina Davenport asked, coming to the door and standing beside her husband's guest. "Come in, come in," she invited, pushing the front door further open for Ellie and gesturing for her to come in.

"Dan said he'd be here shortly. He's running late. Big surprise there, right?" Tina asked with an infectious laugh. She had been a doctor's wife now long enough to take it all in stride without blinking an eye. Tina glanced at her watch. "He did say that if he's not here within fifteen minutes, we should go ahead and start dinner without him."

That didn't seem quite right to Neil. The whole idea of his coming out was to visit with Dan, as well as to help him out with his contrary patient. "Oh no, I can wait," Neil assured his hostess.

"So can I," Ellie said, adding her voice to the doctor's.

"Well, you two might be able to wait," Tina told her dinner guests, "but if I don't feed them," she nodded toward the children who seemed to have just appeared in the room. I could be accused of trying to starve my children."

Tina ruffled her oldest son's hair. The boy wrinkled his nose and, in typical teen fashion, pulled his head back.

"They look pretty healthy and well-fed to me," Neil said, winking at Tina's daughter.

"That's because they can periodically consume their weight in food like hungry little shrews," Tina told her guest. "Good thing they run around as much as they do and wind up burning it off."

Suddenly, her five-year-old perked up, cocking her head to one side and listening. And then she grinned from ear to ear. "Daddy!" the little girl happily cried as she ran from the living room all the way to the front door.

"Jeannie, you know what Daddy and I said about you running to the front door!" Tina warned as she quickly went after her daughter.

"You said *don't*!" Jeannie answered her mother dutifully.

"Sit, I'll go get her," Neil volunteered, on his feet and pursuing his friend's youngest before she could make it to the door.

Because his legs were so long, he was able to catch up to the little girl quickly.

Tina's eyes met Ellie's as she smiled. "I like him," she confided, lowering her voice so that it wouldn't carry any further than just between the two of them.

Ellie tactfully made no comment. She merely smiled in response.

The next moment, there was no need for a reply. Dan's big, booming voice was heard greeting each of his three children. He walked into the living room carrying his youngest in his arms while his middle son had his arms wrapped around his father's leg, apparently hitching a short ride back into the living room.

"And there's my lovely, long-suffering wife," Dan said, setting his daughter down. His son uncurled his body from around his leg while Neil stood back and observed it all. He envied his friend.

"Hi, honey," Dan said, pausing to brush a quick, affectionate kiss on Tina's cheek. "Sorry I'm late," he apologized. His glance swept over his friend, and his guest, as well, the apology meant for all of them. "It just couldn't—"

"—be helped," Tina concluded with a patient, weary smile. "Yes, dear, I know." She glanced toward Neil and Ellie. "That's what he says almost every night," she told them as she walked out of the room. "Dinner will be on the table in five minutes."

"Maybe I should go help her," Ellie said to Dan as she started to follow Tina into the kitchen.

"Don't you dare," Tina called out. "From what

I hear, you work hard enough. Consider this your break."

Dan smiled, his eyes meeting Ellie's. "I'd listen to her if I were you. Tina's one tough little cookie when she wants to be. She likes doing things her way." He chuckled. "I think that comes from having spent some time under Miss Joan's wing when she first came here and settled in Forever," Dan confided to Neil.

Neil shook his head. "This Miss Joan must really be something else," he commented. "I'm really looking forward to finally meeting her."

Hearing him, Ellie laughed in response.

"What's so funny?"

"Nothing," she answered. "Just be careful what you wish for," Ellie told him. She saw Neil's brow rise in a silent question. "Don't get me wrong. Miss Joan is a generous soul, but getting her to see reason can prove to be a very frustrating thing. 'Obedience' isn't a word that's part of her vocabulary—at least not when it's applied to herself," she told Dr. Dan's friend.

Neil looked at Dan for verification. "She's not wrong, you know," Dan assured him.

"Come, sit," Tina urged. "Before everything gets all cold."

Neil followed Tina into the dining room. The

others came behind him. "But she did say that she was willing to see me, right?" he asked Dan.

"What she said," Dan told his friend honestly, having his youngest in tow as he went into the dining room, "was that she 'might' be willing to see a specialist if he came to Forever to see her."

"What is that supposed to mean?" Neil asked. "Is she going to have to be hog-tied before I can conduct any tests on the woman?"

"So you *have* met Miss Joan," Ellie pretended to conclude.

The expression on Neil's face was a cross between confusion and concern. "Are you serious?"

"Ellie is just trying to lighten the moment," Tina explained, giving the pilot a warning look. "Miss Joan isn't that bad. I think her problem is that she just doesn't want to be thought of as being mortal—like the rest of us."

"Personally," Dan interjected, "I think Miss Joan is just afraid that something *might* be wrong and if she submits to these tests, then that fear might be confirmed. If she avoids having the tests, then her fear won't be confirmed."

"But that doesn't change anything," Neil said. "She's just avoiding finding out the truth."

"Treating the woman is going to require patience and understanding—in other words, your lightest touch." Dan nodded. "All right, enough shoptalk," he told the others, rising at the table. He wanted to be in a better position to cut the roast Tina had prepared. "Here, let me cut a piece for you. You'll find that Tina makes a really mean roast and you're going to need some decent red meat to help you face up to dealing with Miss Joan."

"Okay, now you're just exaggerating," Neil said, waving away Dan's prediction. "But I do have a huge weakness for roast beef. It has to be my favorite meal."

"I know," Tina told her guest. She glanced toward her husband. "Dan told me. That's why I made a roast—to celebrate your first visit to Forever."

Neil inclined his head. "I do appreciate that. And the fact that you made mashed potatoes and gravy, as well," he noted, looking at what Tina had set out on the table.

There were a number of bowls, all containing different vegetables that, by the looks of them, had been freshly picked from Tina's garden. In his estimation, Dan was truly a lucky man. His ex-fiancée had never once even attempted to cook for him. The closest Judith had ever come was to order takeout. At the time, he had thought nothing of it, but now he felt that home cooking was a way of displaying affection.

"Tina, everything looks delicious," Neil told his hostess.

"Wait until you taste it," Dan said with pride.

"I can't wait," Neil replied.

"Thank you. I had help." Tina smiled at their guest.

"And by help, she means the kids," Dan told Neil. "I'm afraid that by the time my day is over, all I have the energy for is walking in the door and taking off my shoes." He grinned, adding, "Sometimes not even taking off my shoes."

Neil helped himself to some of the baby carrots, green beans and mashed potatoes. "Remember when you had plans to open a practice on Park Avenue?" Neil reminded his friend.

A faraway smile curved Dan's lips as he nodded at something that sounded like it came from a hundred years ago, or at least another lifetime. "I do."

"Ever wish you had followed through on that?" Neil asked, curious.

To Neil's surprise, Dan never hesitated. He just shook his head. "No. Treating people's imaginary illnesses wouldn't have been nearly as satisfying as the kind of medicine I'm practicing these days.

Granted, a lot less hectic. But it definitely wouldn't have been as satisfying," Dan confided.

"You're serious?" Neil looked directly at Dan. "No regrets?" he asked, studying his friend more closely. "None whatsoever?"

"No," Dan said. "None. My only regret is that there aren't somehow more hours in the day."

"Well, you could achieve that, in a way, by having another doctor working with you at the clinic. I mean, besides Dr. Alisha," Ellie specified, referring to the ob-gyn who had begun working there a few years ago.

Dan chuckled. "I can just see how that ad would read. 'Want to work long hours for very little monetary pay? Compensation would be made in the form of an incredible feeling of well-being and a sense of contribution.'" His eyes met Neil's. "I really don't think that would entice too many people to relocate to Forever." Dan laughed to himself as he thought of his recent communication with Neil. "The only reason I got you to agree to come out here to see Miss Joan was that you felt you needed a change. Now that you're here, you're probably rethinking your decision on the matter."

Neil lifted a shoulder in an evasive half shrug. "Well, we'll see how this all works out," Neil said without committing himself to the situation one way or another. Feeling that the conversation needed a change of pace, he turned his attention to Dan's wife. "The roast beef is really excellent."

"Thank you," Tina replied. "I actually learned how to cook while working at Miss Joan's Diner."

"You worked at Miss Joan's Diner?" Neil asked, surprised.

"I think, at one point or another, most of the young women in town had some sort of a job working at her diner," Tina told him.

Neil looked at Ellie. "But you didn't, right?"

"Actually, I did work there a couple of summers when I was a sophomore and a junior in high school. Pop thought it would be good for me to earn some extra money doing something outside of the family ranch."

Neil rolled the information over in his head. "Your father sounds like a pretty understanding man."

"'Pop' is my grandfather, not my father," Ellie corrected. "But you were right about the other part. He's very understanding."

"Maybe he can talk to this Miss Joan and get her to go along with having those tests done," Neil suggested. And as he said that, another thought occurred to him. "What if it turns out that Miss

Joan is going to need surgery? Even a simple procedure," he pointed out. "What then?"

Dan didn't want to worry about that yet, although he was fairly certain that was going to wind up being the case. "We'll cross that bridge when we come to it," he told his friend.

Neil looked at Dan. "Are you sure we'll be able to?"

"Am I sure?" Dan repeated. "No. Hopeful, yes. You know, I've found that a lot of things that have transpired here in Forever depended entirely on faith. Worrying about how things might turn out too soon never does anyone any good—least of all, me. I've found that I'm at my best when I'm in a positive frame of mind."

Personally, Neil thought, he couldn't operate that way. Obviously, Dan not only operated that way, he seemed to thrive on it. He definitely seemed to be happy about the way his life was going. A great deal happier than Neil was. In a way, he envied Dan.

Tina and Dan made a point to urge Ellie to take Neil outside while they cleared away the dishes and washed them. When Ellie protested that she wanted to help and that it should be Dan who went outside with Neil, the doctor countered her objection.

"This is only a two-person job," Dan said. "Four people will only manage to get in each other's way. Take him outside," Dan instructed Ellie then turned toward Neil. "Go outside and see what it feels like to breathe in some totally decent night air. Ellie, I'm handing him over to you."

Ellie inclined her head and promised agreeably, "I'll try not to lose him. C'mon, this way," she urged the cardiologist.

It took only a few seconds outside of Dan and Tina's house for it to hit Neil. "Wow, it's incredibly dark out here at night."

"I guess this is a far cry from 'the city that never sleeps' for you, right?" Ellie speculated. "There really aren't any lights out here. Once the sun goes down, that's it."

"I never really thought about that," he admitted.

"You have to be really careful out here," she warned him. "One misstep and you can wind up twisting your ankle."

"Maybe I should have brought a flashlight with me—if I had thought to pack a flashlight," he added. When he had agreed to the visit, he hadn't really thought about what he might be getting himself into.

"That's all right, don't worry about it," Ellie assured him. "I've gotten pretty good about being able to see in the dark."

"You're a bat?" Neil asked, amused.

She took his question in stride. "You learn how to compensate. And you also learn how to take very small, measured steps," she added with a grin that Neil was able to hear in her voice rather than actually be able to see.

The next thing Neil knew, she was reaching for his hand. It was a pleasant surprise; one that actually caught him off guard.

She seemed to sense his surprise because she told him, "I'm not getting fresh, Doc. I just don't want to be the one responsible for getting Dr. Dan's friend hurt," she explained good-naturedly.

The simple act of holding her hand like this created a pleasant, warm sensation within Neil that had him totally flummoxed. Slightly embarrassed, he thought he needed to offer some sort of protest. "I'm not that much of a klutz."

Neil had no sooner said the words than Ellie felt a tug on her hand as he came close to tripping over the root of a tree. He would have fallen if she hadn't gripped his hand really hard to keep him upright and on his feet instead of letting him land spread eagle on the ground.

To keep him upright, Ellie instinctively yanked

him toward her. Unprepared, Neil found himself falling into her, their bodies colliding against one another and fitting surprisingly well.

It was hard to say who was the more surprised by what had happened, and which of them ultimately wound up enjoying it more.

Or what happened next.

## Chapter Nine

One moment, Neil was vainly trying not to embarrass himself by tripping in front of the sexy pilot. The next moment, before he actually realized what was happening, he and said sexy pilot were sharing a kiss. "Sharing it" because it was hard to say who kissed whom first—or if there was an instigator responsible for initiating the first move or if this explosive kiss just happened by spontaneous combustion.

However it came to pass, both participants silently agreed that it was more than just an unexpected, exceedingly pleasant surprise.

It was something akin to the first discovery of fire.

At least, Neil felt that way.

When their lips parted and Neil drew his head back, he wasn't even aware that he was grinning from ear to ear—but he was.

"Well, that was certainly unexpected," he murmured when he was finally able to form words.

Ellie's heart was hammering so hard, its beat was practically the only thing she was aware of for several moments. "You'll find that most things that happen in Forever generally are," she told him.

They hadn't even known each other for the span of a day. This wasn't his usually mode of operation and he hardly recognized himself.

"Was I taking advantage of the situation?" he asked Ellie uncertainly.

"Only if you pretended to trip," Ellie told him with a smile.

"No. I hate to admit it, but I really did trip," he admitted, glancing up at the sky. No one ever enjoyed being thought of as a klutz.

"Then, no, you weren't taking advantage of the situation," she said. It surprised her—and also touched her—that he would even think of apologizing.

The sky above was studded with an amazing patchwork of stars. It seemed like the perfect night for two people to get to know one another better, he couldn't help thinking as he looked back at Ellie. "What if I kissed you again?"

"*That* might be viewed as taking advantage of the situation," she told him.

"Then you think that I should trip again first?" Neil asked innocently.

"I think we should be getting back to the house before Dr. Dan and Tina come looking for us and find us sharing more than just an innocent evening stroll." She had no sooner said that than Ellie thought she heard the front door open and Tina calling out to them.

"Ellie, Neil, did you two get lost out here?" Tina asked.

Ellie exchanged looks with Neil. "Speak of the devil," she said to her companion in a low voice, amusement evident in her tone.

Neil raised his voice to answer Tina. "No, we're out here. I'm just noticing how dark everything gets once the sun goes down."

"Quite a culture shock after the bright lights of Broadway," Dan admitted, coming out to join his wife. He slipped his arms affectionately around her waist and pulled her to him.

The next moment, Jeannie burst from the house to join her parents. "Are we playing a game out here?" she asked, eyes wide and hopeful. She was quickly followed by her older brothers. Both seemed just a little more subdued in their comments as they joined the adults.

"Yes, honey," Dan said, putting his hand on his daughter's shoulder to guide her back into the house. "We're playing a game. It's called 'herding your dinner guests back into the house.'" Every word was wrapped in affection.

"All right, you two," Tina announced into the darkness. "Everybody back into the house. My dessert has jelled and is ready to be consumed."

Being young enough to still display enthusiasm over the simpler things in life, Jeannie cheered and clapped her hands together in anticipation. Her older brothers, however, refrained from showing that sort of reaction, although, Neil noted, their pace did pick up a little.

Tina, without a doubt, everyone agreed, made the world's most heavenly desserts.

When dinner and dessert were finally over and it was time for Ellie to leave, Neil insisted on walking her to her vehicle. That freed Dan and Tina to tackle the simpler things in life that they looked forward to: tucking their children into bed and, in Jeannie's case, reading to her until she dropped off to sleep.

The two boys insisted that they were much too old for such "baby things," although they asked to have their door left open so that they could over-hear Dan reading to their sister. As far as Dan was concerned, this was what everything else was all about. It was one of his favorite parts of the day.

"I appreciate you being chivalrous," Ellie told Neil as he walked her the short distance from the Davenport house to her Jeep, "But you really don't have to do this. This isn't the kind of neighbor-hood you're used to," she pointed out, thinking of what she'd heard went on in some New York neighborhoods. "I'm perfectly safe out here walk-ing to my car."

Maybe he was being overly cautious, Neil thought, but that didn't change anything for him.

"Humor me," he told her. "Old habits die hard—and if you're afraid I'm going to use this as an ex-cuse to kiss you again, you don't have to worry," he assured her with a mile. "You're safe."

Ellie cocked her head and peered up into his face. "Are you saying that you don't want to kiss me again?" she deadpanned.

"No, what I'm saying is that…" Neil's voice trailed off as he realized he had managed to paint himself into a corner. "There's no graceful way out of this sentence, is there?"

Ellie grinned at him. "No, not really." Her eyes twinkled in amusement. "Don't worry, Doc. I'm just having a little bit of fun at your expense." And then she grew serious. "So, when are you going to be seeing Miss Joan? Do you have a time yet? Maybe I can sell tickets," she teased.

He looked at her in disbelief, not entirely sure that she *wasn't* serious. "Are you people that hard up for entertainment?"

"Don't sell entertainment short," she quipped, attempting to keep a straight face. And then she told him honestly, "I'm just curious as to who's going to come out the winner here. For Miss Joan's sake, I hope it's you. I wasn't at the diner when Miss Joan nearly passed out," she confided, "but I know some people who were. The upshot of it was that Miss Joan looked frightened. That is not a usual occurrence and *none* of us wants to see her like that again. The woman is the town's rock.

"So," she continued, "if you need a little moral support in bearding the lioness in her den, all you have to do is just say the word and I'm there for you. So are a lot of other people."

Neil thought of the conversation he'd had with Dan when he'd agreed to come to Forever in the first place. "Well, from what I gather, Dan intends for the two of us to go to the diner tomorrow to try to sweet-talk this woman into coming back to the clinic."

Sweet-talking Miss Joan into anything she wasn't entirely sold on doing might prove to be very difficult, Ellie thought.

"She's light enough to be carried if necessary," Ellie pointed out.

Neil laughed at the picture that created. "I think there are laws against forcibly taking a patient in to be examined."

She rolled that over in her mind. "True, but around here, the sheriff enforces the law and Sheriff Rick wants to keep Miss Joan healthy and around just as much as the rest of us do."

Neil nodded. "Maybe she'll surprise us and listen to reason," he speculated.

"Maybe," Ellie agreed. After all, miracles did happen, she added silently as she put her hand on the handle of the Jeep's driver's-side door. "Well, I'd better get going before Pop starts to think I lost my way getting home." She paused for a moment. "If I didn't say it before, Doc, welcome to Forever."

For some reason, Neil couldn't shake the feeling that the words almost sounded like a foreshadowing.

He was letting his imagination run away with him, he thought. The next moment, Neil flashed her a smile. "Thank you."

Opening the driver's-side door, Ellie paused for just a second before getting in. With a quick movement, she brushed a quick kiss against Neil's cheek and then got in behind the steering wheel.

In the blink of an eye, she started up her Jeep and, before he could even process what had just happened, she was gone.

Neil stood there watching her taillights become smaller and smaller until they disappeared completely. He could still feel the warm imprint of her lips on his cheek. Had she kissed him to let him know that she hadn't minded his kissing her earlier? Or because she'd absolved him of that and wanted him to know that they were now even?

Neil lightly glided his fingertips along his cheek as if to press the sensation she'd created there into his skin.

His mouth curved in a slightly bewildered smile.

He was glad that he had come here. He had begun to feel lost and alone after his breakup even though he had been the one to instigate it. He was now beginning to think it was the best thing that had ever happened to him.

The following day, though no one had said a word to Miss Joan about her pending interaction with the cardiologist, somehow she knew.

The moment Dan Davenport and another tall, good-looking man walked through the door into the sacred territory known as Miss Joan's Diner—followed by a few other patrons of the establishment, including Ellie Montenegro—her rail-thin body went on the alert.

Miss Joan raised her hazel eyes up from what she was doing at the counter to hone in on the stranger entering her arena.

She then looked at Dan and nodded, saying, "Hi."

The rest of the diner went deadly silently.

"What can I do for you and your friend, Doc?" she asked in a voice that said she already knew what was coming but wanted to hear them say it.

"You could come back with us to the medical clinic," Dan told her politely.

She looked at him sharply, warily. "And why would I want to do that?"

Dan patiently reminded her of the conversation they'd had the other week. "Because you said you would submit to an examination and tests if I got a cardiologist to come out here to see you."

The expression on Miss Joan's face told Dan she didn't see things that way. "No, I said I'd see him. And, as far as I can tell, that's exactly what

I'm doing right now. I'm *seeing* him," she pointed out, her voice tight.

*This is just wordplay*, Neil thought, and they were wasting time, something he had always felt was a precious commodity.

"Miss Joan—" Neil began patiently.

She turned her eyes on him sharply. "Don't you 'Miss Joan' me, sonny. We haven't even met yet."

Neil suppressed a sigh. "Fair enough," he said, extending his hand to introduce himself. "I'm Dr. Neil Eastwood," he told her.

Miss Joan's eyes narrowed. "Look, Handsome, just because you've got those dimples in your cheeks when you smile doesn't mean that I'm about to peacefully trot off to the medical clinic and let you play doctor with me," she informed him, a warning note in her voice.

"There won't be any 'playing' involved, Miss Joan," Neil respectfully intoned.

With one hand fisted at her hip, Miss Joan gave the man a steely look meant to put him in his place. "Damn straight there isn't going to be any 'playing.' I'm too for you, kid. And too much woman, to boot," she added with a nod of her head. "Now, I've got a diner full of hungry people to feed," she informed him. "So if you don't mind—"

"Oh, but I do mind," Neil said, cutting her short.

"From everything that Dan told me, you are at risk of having a cardiac episode that isn't slanted to have a happy ending if left unattended."

Miss Joan raised her chin defiantly. "Don't you have enough of your own patients to take care of without coming out here, trolling for more?" she asked.

"Yes, I have a lot of patients," Neil agreed. "But, in all honesty, I've never had one the whole town seems to be so worried about."

Miss Joan looked around the diner, glaring at the patrons as if to silently tell them to butt out. "And you still don't. Now, order something or leave," she told him sternly, "because you're taking up space and it's approaching my busiest time of day."

Ellie stepped forward. "What are you afraid of, Miss Joan?"

"I'm not afraid of anything," she snapped a little too sharply.

"All right, then fine…" Ellie said, approaching the counter and Miss Joan. "If you're not afraid, have the Doc run some tests. If he doesn't find anything, everyone's happy and he'll go away." She paused, exchanging looks with Dan. "And if he does find something, he would have caught it early and whatever's wrong can be fixed. Again, everyone's happy."

"I'm not happy," Miss Joan growled.

"You'd rather be sick?" Ellie questioned the older woman.

"I'd rather be left alone," Miss Joan all but barked.

"And you will be, darlin'," Harry, Miss Joan's husband said, adding his voice to the others as he walked into the diner. His eyes never left his wife's face. "Just as soon as you have the tests done."

Miss Joan's angry gaze swept over all the people within the diner. Like a creature backed into a corner, she lashed out.

"Is this the thanks I get after all these years of serving you people, of listening to you whine and complain and giving you a shoulder to lean on? Having you all suddenly decide to gang up on me like this and kicking me when I'm down?" she demanded.

Rather than waste his breath by arguing with the woman, the sheriff, who was also there, told Miss Joan, "Yup," as he came forward. "Now, the sooner you stop being so stubborn, Miss Joan, the sooner you can have these tests done and the sooner you can get back to work," he concluded.

Miss Joan uttered a guttural sound steeped

in frustration. She looked stymied and far from happy at the turn of events. She was usually accustomed to bullying her way out of things as a last resort, but it just wasn't happening this time.

"And my agreeing to this blackmail is the only way I can make you people stop harassing me?" she asked.

"The only way," the sheriff assured her.

"Because we're not going to back off until you submit," Dan told her in no uncertain terms.

Miss Joan thought of something. "You don't have the kind of equipment you need to run these tests," she pointed out. "And I am *not* about to take off to go to some big-city hospital because some cute, big-city doctor thinks he can get me to—"

Neil cut her short before she got too wound up. "I can have whatever's necessary for the tests brought out here," he told her.

Confounded and exasperated, Miss Joan raised her chin defiantly, a fighter looking for a fight. She didn't believe him.

"How?" she challenged.

"I have connections," Neil assured her. "If need be, the necessary equipment for the tests can be flown out here," he told her. "Now, will you say yes?"

"You're not going to stop flapping those gums of yours until I do, is that it?" Miss Joan asked.

Neil held his ground. "That's about it."

Ellie found herself very impressed. She wouldn't have thought the surgeon would stand up to the iron-willed Miss Joan. She'd thought he would back off at the last moment.

"Tell me, when did talking a patient to death become a required course for a medical degree?" Miss Joan asked.

"Since they made you, Miss Joan—and broke the mold," Neil answered. And then he smiled at the crusty woman. "We wouldn't want to risk losing a one of a kind," he told her.

Miss Joan sighed. "I'd better say yes before I wind up in a diabetic coma with all this sweet talk and sugarcoating going on," the woman declared, waving her hand at Neil and, in essence, surrendering. Ever practical, she demanded, "How long are these tests going to take?"

"It'll take up to a day once the necessary equipment comes in," Neil told her.

Rather than say anything to Neil, Miss Joan turned her head toward the kitchen. "All right, I know you heard every word, Angel," she called out to the young woman who did all the cooking. "When these witch doctors are ready to run these voodoo tests of theirs, I'm putting you in charge of my diner."

"Yes, Miss Joan," Angel Rodriguez complacently called back from the kitchen.

"Okay, boys, the ball's in your court," Miss Joan announced to Dan and Neil. "Now, until you get everything here so you can take those damn tests, let me get back to doing my job," she ordered. So saying, she turned her back on the doctors and did just that.

## Chapter Ten

Since she had only come to lend her support and not to actually get anything to eat or drink at the diner, Ellie left.

But she didn't go very far. She hung around because she wanted to tell Neil how impressed she was with the way he had handled Miss Joan. She had seen a lot of people shot down by the dictatorial diner owner.

"Masterfully done," she told the two doctors as they walked out of the diner and down the front steps. "You two handled Miss Joan like pros. Kindly, but firmly," she added with approval.

"Your input helped," Dan told her, grateful she

had thought to show up and add her voice to all the others.

"Yeah, well, we're not exactly home free yet," Neil pointed out.

Ellie put her own interpretation to his words. "You don't think you'll be able to secure the necessary equipment to conduct the tests that you'll need to evaluate her condition?" Ellie asked.

Neil looked at her. Her question had caught him off guard since that wasn't his point.

"Oh, I'm fairly sure I can get what I need. It might take a little doing, but it can be managed," he said, thinking of his network of fellow surgeons.

Confusion creased her forehead. "Then what?" she asked.

Neil voiced his concern to both Dan as well as to Ellie. "I'm thinking beyond that. What if Miss Joan doesn't like the results the tests yield? What if the tests point to her having to have a procedure done, like an angioplasty or an ablation, or something more serious?"

"Like a bypass?" Dan asked.

Neil nodded. "Like that. Then what?"

There was no sense in worrying about what hadn't come to pass yet. "One step at a time," Dan told him. "First, let's get those tests done. Contact those people you know and see what it takes to get everything set up," he advised his friend.

What Neil needed, Ellie thought, was something to divert him. "And after you make those calls and while you're waiting for the equipment to arrive, why don't we see about getting you those driving lessons we talked about?" Ellie suggested.

Well, he hadn't seen that coming, Neil thought. "As I recall, you were the one who did the talking. I just listened."

"But you didn't say no. C'mon, learning how to drive is all part of asserting your independence, Doc," Ellie coaxed. She glanced at Dan for his backing as she continued talking. "Don't you want to come and go as you please?"

The eager pilot was forgetting one crucial point, Neil thought. "To do that, I'd have to have a car," he pointed out.

When he saw the smile that slipped over her lips, he knew that this wasn't going to be his way out of the lessons. "The town mechanic runs a garage," Ellie told him. "I'm sure that he'll be more than happy to set you up with a loaner—provided you know how to drive."

Neil looked toward Dan for help, but his friend was already on his way back to the medical clinic. "You're on your own here, Neil."

Neil sighed. "Are all the women in this town so pushy?" he asked Dan.

Dan laughed. "I'm afraid so, buddy. It's all part of being strong and independent."

"You should have warned me," Neil called after him.

His friend merely smiled at the protest. "Then you wouldn't have come."

"You're right," Neil agreed, raising his voice so that it would carry. "I wouldn't have."

Ellie took hold of his arm, directing Neil toward the clinic. "But you're here now and you might as well make the most of it," she told him. "C'mon, I'll come with you to the clinic and wait while you make those calls to secure the equipment you'll need so you can conduct those tests. And then," she concluded happily, "I'll give you your first lesson."

Neil looked at her skeptically. "I don't know about this…"

"I do," she countered firmly. "And if you're worried about anything happening, Dr. Dan'll treat you at the clinic," Ellie told him. "No waiting," she teased to cinch the argument.

"No waiting," Neil murmured under his breath as if he didn't view that to be a selling feature. Resigned, he decided to go along with this for the time being, but he was far from thrilled. "You know," he told her as they went to the medical clinic, "I've been skydiving a few times."

That surprised her. "Oh?"

"Yes," Neil acknowledged. "And somehow that seemed a lot safer to me than what you're proposing."

"Don't worry," she assured Neil as they approached the clinic directly behind Dan, "I'm not going to have you going any faster in my car than you're totally comfortable with."

Neil gave her an extremely dubious look. "I sincerely doubt that."

To Neil's surprise, after he placed his phone calls to make arrangements for the loan of the medical equipment, the driving lesson went surprisingly well. Contrary to what he had expected, Ellie turned out to be a very patient, very thorough, teacher. She didn't point to any of his shortcomings and set a pace for him that he found exceedingly comfortable. She only went on to the next new point after he had mastered the last one. And although he felt himself having a little difficulty with a couple of the executions, she never once made him feel as if he was failing in the endeavor.

"Okay," Ellie announced as Neil made his way

back to the spot where they had first begun the driving lesson.

"Okay?" he questioned, confused by what she was telling him. For his money, he just felt as if he was getting started.

"Yes. I think you've done enough for one day," Ellie said. In no way was she being judgmental. On the contrary, she sounded as if she was congratulating him.

He looked at her in surprise. "You're kidding," he protested.

Ellie grinned. Things had gone better than she'd hoped and she really felt good about this—as she hoped that he did.

"Doc, you've been driving for almost two hours. You don't want to overdo it." She could see he was about to protest that he wanted to continue. While that made her feel very good about the whole endeavor, she really did need to stop the lesson now. "Besides," she told him, "I have a delivery to make in half an hour and I've got to get ready to leave."

"Are you driving somewhere?" Neil asked. It was hard to miss the hopeful note in his voice. "Because if you are, maybe I can—"

"I'm flying," she told him, cutting Neil's offer short.

"Oh." He looked disappointed, even though he

attempted to cover his reaction. "Well then, I guess I can't come with you."

She surprised him by saying, "Sure you can." She knew he hadn't wanted to hear that, but she teased him by continuing. "There's no passenger on this flight, so you're more than welcome to come along."

"Let me rephrase that," Neil said. "I'd *better* not come. I survived one flight, I don't want to push my luck," he emphasized.

She could only interpret that one way. "You really think I'm going to crash?"

His answer surprised her. "No, I really think I'll embarrass myself and throw up. I narrowly avoided it the last time."

Ellie laughed. Apparently, they had crossed a new threshold when it came to honesty. "I don't think you're giving yourself enough credit, Doc. Besides, how will you ever earn your 'sea legs' if you don't keep challenging yourself?" she asked.

"Hey, dealing with Miss Joan was challenge enough," he told her. That was definitely enough challenge for anyone. "And I did let you take me out for a driving lesson."

Ellie inclined her head, giving him the point. Neil was right. "Sorry, I tend to get greedy when things are going so well," she apologized. "All right, Doc, where do you want me to drop you off before I go pick up the freight for my run?"

That was easy enough to answer. "The medical clinic will be fine—but if you're pressed for time, I can walk there."

She pretended to take offense. "Are you trying to tell me that you don't want my company?"

He stared at her. Where had she gotten that idea? "No, I'm trying to be thoughtful."

And then Ellie smiled at him and he realized that she was pulling his leg. He also realized that he was really getting to like that smile.

"So am I," Ellie said. "Sit tight, Doc. I promise to get you there with no bumps, no bruises, and totally in one piece."

And then she winked.

It was the wink that did it. It alerted Neil that any way he looked at it, this woman was going to be quite a handful. She represented the unexpected and, after being micromanaged to the nth degree by his ex, he had to admit that this was really a pleasant change. A *very* pleasant change. And he welcomed it.

"If you're interested, I'm available for another lesson tomorrow, same time, same place," Ellie told him as she let him out at the medical clinic. "Unless one of your doctor friends come through with that mobile treadmill and that EEG machine by tomorrow."

"I think at the very least it's going to take another day or so," he told her. Then added with a smile, "So, if you're up for a lesson, so am I."

Ellie nodded. "Okay, I'll be here." She beamed at him as he closed the passenger door and turned toward his destination. "You did well today, Doc. Really well."

One compliment deserved another, he thought. And, in his opinion, she had made something he had put off indefinitely seem very easy. "I had a good teacher."

Ellie smiled as she nodded. "Maybe next time, you'll let me teach you how to fly."

"Let's just put a pin in that for a while," Neil told her. There was such a thing as getting too ahead of himself, he thought. Flying a plane had never been on his list of things to do. Ever.

"Oh, but you don't know what you're missing," she told him.

"Yeah, well let's just keep it that way for a while," he told her. Mentally, he added, *For a long while.*

Ellie made no comment. She merely smiled and, he had to admit, though no words were exchanged, her smile did unnerve him.

He honestly didn't know if that was a good thing or not.

\* \* \*

Ellie went ahead and made her run, picking up some much needed supplies from a store located more than seventy-five miles away. The supplies were for Ramona Santiago Lone Wolf, the town's vet.

Driving her ancient station wagon, Mona met Ellie in the open field located just behind her vet facility.

"I appreciate you getting these to me so quickly, Ellie," Mona told her as she got out of her vehicle. "There are times when I really miss Doc Elliott," she said, referring to the old town vet. "I never used to feel that I was operating without a net when he was around. He always seemed to know what to do, what to say. And I could lean on the man," she said wistfully.

Ellie was unloading her plane, piling the supplies on top of one another. She knew exactly how Mona felt. She had the exact same feelings when it came to her grandfather.

"I guess that happens to everyone eventually. It's the way of the world." She smiled at the pretty veterinarian. "Old Doc Elliott must have been an endless source of information for you."

"Oh, for everyone," Mona agreed. "There wasn't anything he didn't know about animals.

Not to mention that the man was also like the town historian. Do you know that he was the only one in Forever who could remember when Miss Joan first came to live here?"

Now that she thought of it, she had heard something to that effect. The woman was so much of a fixture in Forever, it seemed as if she had always lived there.

Ellie paused, trying to remember details.

"Wasn't she married back then?" Ellie asked. "Something about a husband and a baby boy who both died in some sort of a natural disaster, or something like that? A flash flood, I think, was the way the story went." As she talked, bits and pieces of details came back to her. "That's why she was so closed off for so long and why it took Harry more than thirty years to convince her to marry him.

"That would almost be romantic if it wasn't so sad," Ellie commented. With a mighty effort, she deposited the last of the supplies from her plane onto the ground.

"If I remember it correctly, it wasn't a flash flood, it was a car accident," Mona told her. "Miss Joan's husband was pretty much of a scoundrel and he ran off with Miss Joan's sister. Zelda or Zoë or something like that," she said, totally surprising

Ellie. "Doc Elliott said that her husband took the baby because he was trying to get back at Miss Joan for giving him such a hard time. As if anyone would applaud a womanizer," the woman said in disgust.

"And they were killed in a car accident?" Ellie asked, still attempting to absorb the information. In all the years she had lived in Forever, she had never heard this story. She was still a little doubtful about how true it was. Not that she didn't believe Mona, but it just seemed so unusual that there was never any mention of it. "Are you sure about this?" she pressed.

Mona nodded as her voice took on a somber tone. "The baby died instantly. Miss Joan's husband lingered for a few days before succumbing to his injuries."

"And the sister?" Ellie asked, stunned by this revelation.

"Not a scratch," Mona declared. "She was the one who was driving."

Ellie felt almost numb. She tried to reconcile the information with the woman she had known all her life. "How awful." She couldn't help ask, "How come I've never heard any of this before?"

"Out of respect for Miss Joan," Mona told her, "Doc Elliott didn't want the story getting around."

Okay, she could understand that. But something else was bothering her. "So then why did he tell you?" she asked. It didn't seem to make any sense.

"He told me because he thought it might help me out. I was going through a tough time. I won't go into any of the details," Mona told Ellie, "but suffice it to say that it did help. And, out of respect for Doc Elliott, I never told anyone."

"Until now?" Ellie questioned. Again her curiosity was raised. "Why say anything now?"

That was simple enough to explain. "Because sometimes secrets can eat up our insides. I think that maybe it would do Miss Joan some good to own up to this. Maybe she can even finally call a truce with her sister."

"A truce?" Ellie questioned. This seemed to be getting more and more involved.

"Yes, according to what Doc Elliott told me. When her sister came to see Miss Joan to try to tell her how very sorry she was for everything that had happened… How she would give anything if none of it had ever happened…" Mona then repeated in an aside, "Like I said, Miss Joan's husband was a scoundrel and he turned her sister's head and talked her into running off with him." Then concluded, "Miss Joan told her to get out. That she never wanted to see her again."

"And did she?" Ellie asked. She couldn't imagine never speaking to her own sister, no matter what Addie might be guilty of doing.

"Nope," Mona answered. "Not that anyone ever knew about any of this. I mean, nobody but me even knew she had a sister, and that was just because of what Doc Eliott told me. The woman left town a long time ago. From what Doc Elliott told me, the story died down, time passed and Miss Joan just became the Miss Joan we know today."

"How do you know this even happened?" Ellie questioned.

"Because Doc Elliott wasn't the type to make things up, even for a good cause, like to help me deal with things." Mona took in a breath. She had spent enough time in the past. "All right, let's get this all back to my clinic and I'll settle up with you there. I've got horses to treat if I don't want this thing to spread and we wind up with a full-fledged epidemic on our hands."

Ellie nodded but, unlike the sheriff's sister, her mind wasn't on sick horses. She was still focused on what Mona had told her.

"You want me to keep this between us, Mona?" she asked the vet.

Mona thought the matter over for a moment.

"Actually, you do what you think is best. Maybe

it's about time someone go looking for Miss Joan's sister and, if she'd still alive, bring her back here so that fences can be mended. I'd say that thirty or more years is definitely enough time to have passed." She looked at Ellie. "Don't you think?"

"Oh, more than enough time," Ellie agreed, nodding her head.

She couldn't wait to get home to tell Pop about this new-old development.

## Chapter Eleven

Ellie went over what she wanted to say to her grandfather a number of times in her head as she drove back to the ranch. But when she finally arrived and found him in the tack room, she could only blurt out, "Pop, how long have you lived in Forever?"

Eduardo was focused on repairing an old, beloved saddle whose leather had become extremely worn in places. Ellie had offered to buy him a new one, but he had turned her down. Not because he hadn't wanted her to spend the money but because the saddle had a great many memories associated with it. Too many to mention, or recreate, he'd mused.

Surprised by the question, Eduardo looked up.

"You know the answer to that as well as I do, Ellie. I came here when you were six and Addie was four. Your father and mother had just gotten into that terrible car accident." He set down his tools and gave his granddaughter his full attention. "Being notified about that accident had to be the very worst day of my life. But that day became the best day of my life because that was the day I became the guardian of two precious little girls."

The events were foggy and jumbled in her head, but Ellie could still remember some things. "I remember that Miss Joan came and got us in the middle of the night. She took Addie and me to her place, right?"

"Right." Eduardo studied his granddaughter, wondering why she was asking after all this time had passed. "Where is this going, Ellie?"

She wanted to get a few things straight first before she went on to tell Pop what she had found out. "There wasn't anyone else living with her at the time, was there?" She didn't remember that there was, but she could have been mistaken.

"No, there wasn't." Eduardo rose from the seat

where he was sitting and faced his granddaughter. "Again, where is this going?"

Rather than beat around the bush, Ellie decided to dive into the subject headfirst. "Did you know that Miss Joan has a sister?"

Eduardo frowned slightly, the lines in his forehead deepening. "No, you're mistaken. I heard that she had a son, a toddler actually, and a husband. They both died in some sort of flash flood many years ago, but as far as I know, no one has ever asked her about it and she never volunteered any information. I certainly never heard about a sister. Why?" He cocked his head, looking at his granddaughter intently. "What did you hear and who did you hear it from?" he asked. He knew that gossip was alive and well in Forever, as well as thriving here some of the time.

Ellie didn't want to name names yet. "I got it from a very reliable source who heard it from someone she trusted—"

"Ah, third-hand information." Eduardo nodded knowingly. His eyes narrowed slightly. "You know what I think of that sort of thing, Ellie."

"Yes, I know, but there has to be some way that we can check this out, some sort of records that can be accessed to see if this information can be verified," she insisted. "It *might* be true," she stressed, more than willing to give the possibility of Miss Joan having a sister the benefit of the doubt.

Eduardo gave his granddaughter's question some thought. "Well, you could try asking the sheriff's wife, Olivia, to look into the matter. She's a family lawyer and, if anyone would know how to access this kind of information, she would. But this seems very important to you—why now?"

"Pop, Miss Joan might be facing a medical crisis...and you know her. If it comes to that, if she needs an operation and has to go to a hospital to get it, she's not going to want to hear about it. If she has family somewhere, like a sister, and we could find that person, maybe she could talk Miss Joan into having the procedure done," Ellie argued.

"Ellie, you are presupposing that she is going to need surgery and that she is going to refuse to have it done," Eduardo said. "Miss Joan is not a stupid woman," he reminded his granddaughter. "Why don't we just wait and see what those tests tell the doctor?"

That was simple enough to answer. "Because I don't like waiting to the last minute. I believe in being prepared. I always have."

Eduardo shook his head and laughed softly under his breath. "Lord, but you are your father's daughter," he said fondly. "He was always obsessing over things like that when he was your age, too."

Ellie liked hearing that she had something in common with her father. For the most part, both of her parents were mere shadows in her memory. And that only made her that much more committed to following through on this new mission she had set up for herself.

Miss Joan had been there for her and for her sister, even though Addie had no memory of the time. As for her, Ellie could actually remember Miss Joan coming into her home and telling her and her sister that they were going to be staying with her for a while. When she had asked why, Miss Joan had gathered the two of them onto her lap, held them close for a moment and said that they were going to be with her until their grandfather came for them. She was the one who'd broken the news to them that her parents had "gone to heaven."

Ellie vividly remembered the scent of cinnamon when Miss Joan had given them the news and she remembered seeing tears in the woman's eyes as she'd spoken.

Beyond that, there were only disjointed bits and pieces floating through her mind. But Ellie knew she owed the older woman a great deal.

Looking back now, knowing what she had just

learned, Ellie realized that Miss Joan had been re-living her own tragedy because of what had happened to her and Addie.

If there was even the tiniest possibility that any of old Doc Elliott story was true, Ellie owed it to Miss Joan to track down what had happened to the mystery sister. She couldn't shake the feeling that this might actually help things in the long run—as long as that sister were still alive.

"Thanks, Pop," she said. "I'm going to go see if I can catch Olivia in her office." With that, she walked out of the tack room.

Eduardo nodded. "Let me know if there's anything I can do," he called after her.

"I will," she promised. *Provided there is anything to be done*, she added silently.

Ellie rehearsed what she was going to say to Olivia at least three times before she got to the woman's law office in the middle of Forever. As it turned out, when Ellie told the woman about her discovery, Olivia was surprised, to say the least.

After listening to Ellie repeat the whole story, the family lawyer was silent for several seconds then said, "Well, I can definitely look into this for you. I have a few ideas where I could try to find out if there's any truth at all to the information.

Do you want me to let Cash in on this?" she asked since Cash Taylor was not only her law partner, he was also Miss Joan's husband's grandson. Olivia assumed, because Cash hadn't said anything to her, that he was in the dark about this, as was his grandfather.

"Well, if this does turn out to be true," Ellie said, knowing that Olivia was a little skeptical, though for her, the feelings that it was true were growing stronger and stronger, "then he and Harry are going to need to be filled in eventually."

"You know how private Miss Joan is," Olivia pointed out. "She might not like anyone knowing. If this does turn out to be true, there's a reason no one's ever heard about it."

"I know. But I'm willing to bet that nobody in town likes the idea of living in a world without Miss Joan if we can possibly help it. And something tells me that we might need a lot of ammunition on our side to convince that woman to agree to have the surgery—if that does turn out to be the case," Ellie amended.

Olivia nodded. "You have a point. I'll get on this right away," she promised. "But if I hit a wall, then I'm going to ask Cash for help," she warned.

Ellie nodded. "Sounds fair." And then she got down to practical matters. "Look, I can't pay you up front, Olivia, but maybe we can come up with some sort of a weekly arrangement so that—"

Olivia looked at Ellie, a somber expression on her face. "Are you trying to insult me?"

Ellie stared at her. "No, of course not. Why would you even ask something like that?"

Olivia drew herself up in her chair, her posture military-rigid. "Because you're making it sound as if you have a monopoly when it comes to caring about Miss Joan—and you don't," the woman informed her. "Miss Joan, whether she likes it or not, is community property. *All* of us owe her something. *All* of us care about the woman because, for one reason or another, at one time or another, Miss Joan was there for each and every one of us when we needed her most."

Ellie smiled at the lawyer who had hit the matter right on the head. "I didn't intend any disrespect, Olivia."

Olivia nodded her head. "I know that, but sometimes things need repeating." She looked down at the notes she had made to herself while Ellie had told her what she knew. "I'll let you know as soon as I find something—and, Ellie," she called after the pilot who was already at the door, ready to leave.

Ellie turned around, waiting.

"Good call," Olivia told her. "I've got a feeling we're going to need everything we can gather together in our arsenal to get that sharp-tongued, stubborn old woman to listen to reason."

Ellie smiled at Olivia and nodded. "I know."

Ellie wanted to tell Neil about this latest potential development with his patient, but she was forced to wait until the following day when they were to meet for the doctor's next driving lesson.

She swung by the Davenport house that following morning to pick him up. Ellie fully intended to tell him about Miss Joan's possible mystery sister the moment she saw him. But Neil looked so anxious to get behind the wheel for another driving lesson that she decided to put her news on hold. It could keep until another couple of hours had passed.

"You know, I am really surprised that you never decided to do this on your own," she told Neil after he very neatly parked her Jeep in the spot she had pointed out. The man, she thought, was a natural. "You're really good at it."

He almost beamed in response to her compliment. "Thanks. But I honestly never wanted to before." He tried to make her see it from his point of view. "Between taxis, buses and trains, there was never any need for me to learn. You teaching me has put a whole different spin on things," he confided. "For one thing, you make it look like fun."

They were parked over to the side of a road and there was no one else around. Alone like this with her had Neil feeling all sorts of romantic inclinations again. "You make a lot of things look like fun," he confessed.

Despite the fact that the Jeep was opened up, Ellie suddenly felt a lot warmer.

She was allowing herself to be distracted, she upbraided herself, and right now, as drawn to Neil as she felt, she couldn't afford that to happen. "I have some news about Miss Joan for you."

She caught him off guard, but he had his own news and he had a feeling that his was better. "So do I, actually. One of the people I went to medical school with went into the same branch of medicine I did and, after he graduated, he relocated not too far from this section of Texas.

"I kind of got him through medical school," he added, "and he feels he owes me, which in this case is a good thing. When I contacted him, he agreed to let me borrow the equipment I need to conduct Miss Joan's tests and assess the results. Everything I need will be here by tomorrow. I'll have to work fast because the loan is only for the day—but that should give me more than enough time to ascertain if Miss Joan has some sort of coronary issue going on or not."

Finished with what he had to tell Ellie and happy things were going so well, Neil asked, "All right, what's your news?"

"I found out that Miss Joan might have a sister," Ellie said.

He wasn't sure why that would be viewed as good news one way or another.

"Well," he allowed slowly, "I suppose that's good news in case Miss Joan winds up needing a kidney, but otherwise—"

Ellie realized that he didn't see the possible problem this sort of news could very well avert. She filled him in.

"This might be the person we need to help tip the scales in case you do need to operate on Miss Joan. The woman can be exceptionally stubborn and maybe the promise of being reunited with an estranged relative might be what we need to get her to agree to having the surgery."

"You really believe that?" he questioned. "That turning up with this so-called 'mystery' person will make her listen to reason?"

"I *have* to believe that," Ellie told the surgeon. "Sometimes faith is all we have to get us through things. I believed that Dr. Dan would find a way to get a cardiologist to come take a look at Miss Joan and here you are," she grandly announced.

Neil laughed, shaking his head. "I don't know how to argue with that."

"Then don't," she told him. "There's no point in arguing, anyway."

"Say, would you like to come with me to the diner so we can tell Miss Joan the news?" he asked, feeling that if Ellie was so involved in this, she should be there for the highlights.

She wasn't sure what he was referring to. "About finding out that she has a sister, or about the necessary lab equipment coming tomorrow morning?"

"Why don't we tell her about the latter and hold off telling her the other news until this 'sister' is actually located and on her way here?" Neil suggested. "Think of it as our possible ace in the hole."

She thought of that as an unusual way for him to phrase it. "You play poker, Doc?"

Amused, Neil smiled at her. "On occasion."

"I would have thought that someone like you would prefer playing a more cerebral game, such as bridge or chess."

He didn't want Ellie harboring a stuffy image of him. "Actually, I find poker to be more down-to-earth and exciting," he told her. "Maybe while I'm here, after everything is over with, you and I can play a hand or two."

Ellie smiled at the thought. "Maybe," she agreed. "But right now, I think you should tell Miss Joan to get ready for those tests tomorrow. By the way, did I hear you right? Did you say something about your friend shipping out a portable treadmill machine?"

He nodded. "You heard right," Neil told her.

That was both good and bad. Good, because it was obviously necessary and bad because… "She's not going to be thrilled about that."

"I don't need her to be thrilled," Neil said. "I just need her to agree to do it."

"Isn't that test for younger people?" Ellie questioned, anticipating Miss Joan's reaction.

"It's for anyone with a heart who is able to walk," Neil told her. "And from what I've observed, Miss Joan can not only walk, she can get around rather fast for a woman her age."

Ellie raised her hand to stop him. "Word of advice."

Curious because he hadn't said anything that unusual, he said, "Go ahead."

She couldn't keep the grin off her lips. "If you want to stay alive, I'd stay away from using terms like 'a woman your age' when talking to Miss Joan unless you want to observe being vivisected up close and personal by a layperson."

Neil laughed, waving his hand at her advice. "I'm sure that Miss Joan's bark is worse than her bite."

"I wouldn't put even money on that if I were you," Ellie told him.

Neil read between the lines. "She means a lot to you, doesn't she?"

Ellie saw no reason to deny it. "Miss Joan is the closest thing that Addie and I have to a mother. You'll find that a lot of people in this town feel that way."

Neil nodded. That was becoming very clear to him. "Then I'll be sure that all the tests are performed carefully and correctly," he promised. "Now, let's go and beard the lioness in her den."

"You drive," Ellie told him, remaining seated where she was.

Her suggestion pleased him. He felt like a student who had just graduated after taking an accelerated program. "All right," he said, restarting the engine, "I will."

## *Chapter Twelve*

Ellie was thoroughly convinced that Miss Joan had some sort of special radar that managed to alert her to things, even though it didn't seem really possible.

Despite the fact that the diner was relatively full and she wasn't even remotely looking in their direction, somehow the woman just seemed to know the moment they walked in.

Setting down a pair of menus in front of two of her patrons seated at the counter, Miss Joan didn't even look Ellie and Neil's way when she asked, "You two here to eat, or did you come for the sole purpose of bending my ear?"

To his credit, Neil recovered from the unexpected confrontation first. "A little of both," he answered truthfully.

Miss Joan moved over to the couple. "Well, if you're here to eat, you're more than welcome to sit down because, after all, that's the business I'm in. But if you're here to use that as an excuse just to bend my ear and try to talk me into something, you know where the door's located," she told them. "And just in case you forgot—" Miss Joan gestured toward the door "—there it is."

Neil looked at Ellie. "You in the mood for steak?" he asked. Then, before she had a chance to answer, Neil made the decision for them; he needed leverage to use with Miss Joan. If they were eating her food, then she had to be more receptive to what he was saying. "We'll take two of your finest steaks."

Miss Joan gave him a withering look, as if he should know better. "There is no 'finest.' All the steaks here are good, sonny."

Neil never missed a beat. "Then it shouldn't be any trouble picking out two of them for us," Neil told her. "I like mine rare. How about you, Ellie? How do you like your steak?"

"Tasting like a chicken," she answered.

Neil looked at her, confused. "What?"

Rather than explain it to him, she looked at Miss Joan. "You have any of that fried chicken you had on the menu the other day?"

"We might," Miss Joan answered evasively. Then, because it was Ellie, she warmed up a little. "I'll have Angel check. If she doesn't have any, she can whip up a batch. That okay with you?" Miss Joan asked.

That would definitely give Neil more time to talk to the woman, Ellie thought as she slanted a glance at Neil. "That'll be perfect," she told the woman.

"What do you want to go with that?" Miss Joan asked the duo, pretending that she believed they were there for lunch.

"Whatever you pick will be fine," Ellie said, determined to be easy.

Neil nodded in agreement. "What she said."

Miss Joan planted herself directly in front of them, one fisted hand on her waist. "Okay, now you two are just trying to butter me up. Just what are you really after?" she asked.

"A really good meal," Ellie returned guilelessly. "Doc here thinks that New York diners have cornered the market when it comes to serving really great, inexpensive meals, and we know better than that, don't we, Miss Joan?" she asked in a conspiratorial voice.

Miss Joan's frown went clear down to the bone. "You must think I was born yesterday," she accused.

"No, we don't," Ellie protested, deliberately assuming a wide-eyed expression.

"But you do look young enough to pass for that," Neil said innocently, tongue in cheek.

Miss Joan's eyes narrowed as she gave him a piercing look. "Don't try to flirt with me, sonny," she warned the cardiologist.

"I wouldn't dream of it," Neil told her. And then his voice turned more serious. "But I am going to tell you that my friend came through."

"Good for you," Miss Joan responded cryptically. "Your orders will be up very soon," she told them as she began to walk away.

Neil rose a little in his seat as he called after her. "What time will be good for you?"

Turning, Miss Joan studied him for a long moment then said, "That all depends. Good for what?"

Okay, this had gone on too long, Ellie thought. The doctor's patience could only be pushed so far before he lost it. She answered for him. "To do the tests he came out here to do, Miss Joan."

Miss Joan raised her chin a little. "What if I say 'never'?"

Ellie looked at the woman in surprise. This was something new. "Miss Joan, you can't go back on your word."

"Sure I can," she contradicted. Asserting herself, Miss Joan said, "I can do anything I damn well please. I haven't had another one of those fluttery incidents since the baby doctor here arrived in town."

"Doesn't mean it's not going to happen again," Neil pointed out. "And having the proper equipment shipped out here like this is the most convenient I can make it for you."

"That's not true," Miss Joan replied, her eyes meeting his. "It would be more convenient for you to forget about this whole thing altogether. So how about it?"

Ellie answered for him, feeling that since she'd known Miss Joan a lot longer, she was in a better position to become tough with the older woman. "I can get Harry and Cash to strong-arm you," Ellie told the woman.

Hazel eyes held Ellie prisoner.

"You can get them to *try*," the older woman informed her haughtily.

Ellie's voice softened as she tried another approach. "Miss Joan, you mean a great deal to all of us. Please, please just agree to go along with having these tests done," she pleaded. "Who knows, maybe you will be in the clear once they're done and then everyone can drop this whole subject."

The expression on Miss Joan's face was dubious, but she threw up her hands in exasperation. "All right, all right! I'll have the damn tests done—and *then* we *will* drop the whole subject," she declared.

*Maybe*, Neil added silently. "All right, how does tomorrow morning at 9:00 a.m. sound?" He reasoned that everything would have arrived and been set up in Dan's office by then.

"Lousy," Miss Joan answered honestly.

Neil glossed right over that. "If we get started by nine, we should be finished before your noon rush hour starts," he proposed.

Unwilling to commit, Miss Joan just shrugged. "We'll see."

Neil frowned. "Miss Joan—" he said, a warning note in his voice.

She blew out an exasperated breath. "All right, all right! If it gets you people off my back, I'll be there tomorrow at nine."

"Why don't I come by the diner and pick you up?" the doctor proposed.

Miss Joan pretended to take offense at the suggestion. "You don't trust me?"

Neil smiled at her. "No further than I can throw you," he answered good-naturedly.

Miss Joan actually chuckled under her breath at that. "You're smarter than you look, sonny. I'll go see how Angela is doing with your order," she announced, slipping into the small kitchen.

As she walked away, Neil caught a glimpse of Ellie beaming at him. "What?"

"Nicely played, Doc," she said. "I think Miss Joan actually respects you."

"I think that just might be Miss Joan's way of accepting the inevitable," Neil pointed out. "She's an intelligent woman. I think she knows that she can only put this off for so long."

Ellie laughed at his naïveté, which she found adorable. "Miss Joan knows no such thing. You have no idea how far that woman can push her unique brand of stubbornness. At bottom, the only thing I can hope for is that, worse comes to worst, everyone will gang up on her and force that woman to agree." She wasn't even thinking as far as having an actual procedure performed. "Well, at least she's agreed to submit to the tests."

Neil eyed her knowingly. He knew that they were both thinking the same thing. "Unless she changes her mind by tomorrow," he sighed, shaking his head. Why had he even gotten himself into this? Since he had, he was now committed. "We're just going to have to make sure she doesn't."

"Do you need a hand getting everything set up at the clinic?" Ellie asked, more than ready and eager to help out in any way possible.

"As it turns out, I've got a lot of volunteers," Neil told her. That, in turn, had surprised him. He wasn't accustomed to such a communal effort. "You're right. Everyone really cares about Miss Joan." He paused, reflecting for just a second. "This is a really nice place."

And then, just like that, he changed his focus, moving on to something more personal. "You know, I could use some company tonight," he told her, taking her up on her offer to help out.

She thought she heard something in his voice, something he wasn't aware of. "Are you nervous?"

He backed off a little. "No." Then he told her, "But I still wouldn't mind some company. If you're not doing anything," he qualified.

Ellie was about to answer him, but the sheriff chose that moment to come up behind them. He placed a friendly hand on Neil's shoulder, isolating Neil's attention and turning it toward him.

"I'm afraid we've got other plans for you,

Doc," Rick told him, surprising both Neil and Ellie, as well.

Neil turned on his stool and gave the sheriff a curious look. "What kind of plans?"

It had taken some preparation and coordination, but Rick made it sound as if it had all been spontaneous and spur of the moment.

"Well, the Murphy brothers are throwing a little party in your honor at Murphy's tonight," he said as if he and Dan hadn't been the ones to get the ball rolling. "And it won't be much of a party if you don't attend."

"A party?" Neil echoed, surprised at the whole idea. Had he missed something? "Nobody said anything about a party."

"That's because this was all just one of those last-minute deals, just like these tests for Miss Joan," the sheriff explained. And then Rick smiled. "It's our way of saying thanks for coming out all this way to see the cantankerous woman and going through all this extra trouble to make sure that she's going to be around for a long while.

"Yes, Miss Joan," Rick said as Miss Joan came out of the kitchen and gave him what passed for a dark look, "we are talking about you."

"Well, stop it. Unless you don't want to keep on

eating here," she warned. "And since this the only place in town where you can get a decent meal—"

"—at least one you have to pay for," Ellie said, adding her two cents and earning a dour look from the woman.

Rick knew that Miss Joan had overheard everything—he firmly believed the woman had ears like a bat—so he didn't bother repeating himself or attempting any sort of a further explanation.

"You're welcome to come, too, you know. As long as you promise to leave that viper tongue of yours home, Miss Joan."

"Meaning you want me to keep quiet? Humph. What fun would that be?" she challenged.

Laughing under his breath, the sheriff looked at Neil. "I sure don't envy you, Doc. You're going to have your work cut out for you tomorrow with this one," Rick predicted. "That's part of the reason the Murphys thought you might appreciate attending a party tonight." It was also, he added silently, the main criteria behind having it now rather than later. "Six o'clock work for you?"

He'd had a totally different, more intimate sort of evening in mind, but this could work, too, Neil thought. He was rather flattered by the gesture, actually. However, he didn't want to presume too much.

"You really don't have to do all this, you know," he told the sheriff.

"Sure we do," Rick said. "Tell him, Ellie." The sheriff turning to her for backup.

"What he's trying to tell you…" she explained, wondering why the sheriff would think it would sound any better coming from her, "is that what we lack in volume, we more than make up for in enthusiasm." She took a quick breath. "Like I said, everyone cares about everyone else if you're part of Forever." She thought for a moment then decided that maybe this would bring it home for Neil. "It took Dr. Dan a while to get used to that idea. But once he did—" she smiled "—there was literally no going back for him. And thank goodness, because we needed him as much as he needed us. Still," she allowed, "Forever isn't for everyone." She didn't want him to think she was attempting to railroad him into something. "There have been people born here who couldn't *wait* until they were old enough to get away. Some of them, though," she had to add honestly, "eventually did come back."

"Well, right now I'm just going to go to the party and enjoy myself—within reason," Neil qualified. When she looked at him quizzically, he explained. "Something tells me I'm going to need all my wits about me for tomorrow when I'm conducting those tests on Miss Joan."

Ellie nodded her head in agreement. "You really are a quick study."

After the impromptu early lunch, they both went their separate ways: Neil to consult with Dan and Ellie to the ranch to tell her grandfather and sister about the party that was being thrown at Murphy's.

It had been a while since her grandfather had socialized with his neighbors and she knew he could use the diversion. As for her sister, she knew that Addie was always up for a party. If she found out that Ellie hadn't told her about it, she would have been one very unhappy sister and an unhappy Addie was not something that any of them could easily put up with.

Besides, she knew that Addie wanted to meet this new doctor and, even though she found herself getting more and more attracted to him, far more than she thought she would be, Ellie definitely didn't want Addie thinking she was attempting to hide the man from her.

"A party?" Pop questioned when she told him. "For this doctor friend of Dr. Dan?"

Ellie nodded. "It's to say thanks. I think it was the sheriff's idea. Rick's and the Murphy brothers," she added, spreading the credit around. "I think they're hoping that if they do everything they can to make it hospitable for the Doc, he'll keep that in mind when he's dealing with Miss Joan." She smiled at her grandfather, her voice filled with affection. "We all know she can be pretty rough on a person if they're not used to her ways," Ellie said.

"Well, I don't care what the reason is, I'm always up for a party," Addie said, listening.

"And here I thought you wouldn't want to go," Ellie deadpanned.

Addie looked at her sister as if she had grown another head and then waved a dismissive hand. "Very funny, El. Ha, ha." She then turned to her grandfather. "So, do we all go together, or should I drive in separately?" she asked, a hopeful note in her voice.

"Why don't we all go together?" Pop suggested. "Like a family."

"Works for me," Ellie agreed.

"Yeah, me, too," Addie said with a sigh that belied the truth behind her words.

## Chapter Thirteen

In the end, Ellie did wind up taking her own vehicle to the party at Murphy's. She had forgotten all about an errand she'd needed to run and hadn't wanted to make Pop and Addie arrive at Murphy's late just because she would be.

By the time she arrived at the family type saloon, the parking had quickly filled with vehicles and the air resounded with the music that Liam, the professional musician in the Murphy family, was performing with his band.

Ellie could feel the music before she even got out of her Jeep.

Entering the packed establishment, she quickly

scanned the immediate area to see if Neil had arrived yet. He had, as had Miss Joan, who was there with her husband, Harry. Besides Harry, there were several other people milling around the diner owner.

Ellie realized from the evident body language that this was a party with a duel purpose. It was to say "thank you" to the cardiologist going way out of his way to ensure Miss Joan's health and it was for Miss Joan, as well, to show the woman how loved she was by everyone and how much she meant to the people of Forever.

If it turned out that Olivia wasn't able to locate Miss Joan's mystery sister, Ellie hoped this would be enough to cement the argument that Miss Joan couldn't just blatantly ignore the test results if they wound up pointing to her needing surgery. Her life wasn't her own to do with whatever she chose to do with it. Like it or not, her life belonged to all of them.

Spotting her family, Ellie waved at Pop. When he saw her, Eduardo immediately waved back. He was busy talking to Julia Anderson, recently widowed in the last year. Addie, as usual, was in the center of a group of young men. The girl was a regular walking–guy magnet. Ellie would have been worried about her sister if it wasn't for the fact that Pop kept such a sharp eye on her.

Too sharp in Addie's opinion, Ellie mused, but any young man who was worth her attention would easily endure Pop's scrutiny. It was a small price to pay to have a vivacious young woman in their life.

"I see you finally made it."

Ellie nearly jumped when she heard the deep voice behind her.

Between the loud, throbbing, pulsating music and her own thoughts, Ellie hadn't heard anything, least of all Neil coming up behind her until he was right there, less than an inch away.

Startled, she had to catch her breath as she swung around to face him. "You know, if you ever get tired of being a surgeon and decide to take up a second career, you might give cat burglary a try. You've got sneaking up on people down pat."

He laughed. "How long have you been this jumpy?"

"How long have you been in town?" she countered archly.

A deep smile curved his lips. "Should I be flattered?"

The noise level had increased again, drowning out his words. Ellie was forced to point to her ear and shake her head to let him know she hadn't heard what he'd just said.

Leaning in, Neil tried again, this time whispering the words directly into her ear. "Should I be flattered?" he repeated.

The warmth of his breath curled along her neck and cheek, and Ellie had to struggle not to shiver in response. It was even more of a struggle to attempt to keep her wits about her and not go with the gut reaction that made her want to kiss him.

From out of the blue, a sadness took hold of her. They were just getting to know one another, with the promise of so much more, but he would be leaving soon. And then what?

She had no answer.

"You can be anything you want to be," Ellie finally responded. Desperate to change the subject, she looked around the crowded saloon again, hoping to have something present itself.

"What are you looking for?" he asked. Again, he was forced to bring his mouth close to her ear so that she would hear what he was asking her.

Ellie raised her voice as she answered him. "I know that the Murphys and Miss Joan have an agreement about who serves what at their separate establishments, but I thought that since she was attending this party here, she might have brought some food with her."

Rather than say anything, Neil took her arm and directed her attention to a table set up in one of the far corners. It was loaded with all sorts of quick snacks. There were platters of tiny quesadillas, enchiladas and small, edible flour "baskets" filled with salads comprised of three kinds of peppers, tomatoes and shredded Romaine lettuce. There was also a mouthwatering selection of three kinds of meat.

"For snacking," he explained. "If the Murphys and Miss Joan ever decide to join forces and form one large establishment, nobody is ever going to get any work done again," Neil predicted.

She laughed. "You're probably right."

Rather than head over to the table, Ellie turned on her heel and went in the complete opposite direction.

"I thought you said you were hungry," Neil said. "Why aren't you getting something to eat?"

"No, I asked if Miss Joan had brought any food. I was just curious. I can eat later," she assured Neil. "Right now, they're playing one of my favorite songs," she told him, cocking her head to listen as she allowed the beat to get into her hips and direct them. "Do you dance?"

"Not well enough to put me on Broadway," he answered. "But yes," Neil acknowledged, "I do."

That was when she presented herself to him by putting out her hands in a silent invitation to dance. "I happen to know there are no talent agents here tonight, scouting Murphy's, so you're in the clear. You don't have anything to be embarrassed about."

Neil grinned warmly at her, his eyes sparkling. "Well then, I guess I have no excuses left."

And with that, he slipped one arm around Ellie's waist, took hold of her hand with his other hand, and proceeded to dance with her to the heart-racing tempo.

When the number ended—and Ellie felt as if she had just covered the entire floor three times over—the band struck up another song, the beat even more compellingly arousing.

Neil cocked his head, his eyes silently asking her if she wanted to continue dancing. When Ellie smiled her response, her eyes crinkling, it was all that he needed. The next number started and he didn't even bother asking her. They just continued dancing.

But after the third dance ended, Ellie held up her hand and cried, "Uncle!" as she struggled to catch her breath.

Neil pretended to take her literally. He scanned the immediate area as he asked, "Where?"

Ellie didn't answer that. Instead, she just told him, in small gasps, "I think I need some air."

Neil dropped the pretense. He nodded and, taking her hand in his, led Ellie outside as if he were the town native and she the visitor.

"Fortunately," he responded, "fresh air is something that Forever seems to have in absolute abundant supply." He pushed open the door and the difference was immediately evident.

The rush of cool air felt wonderful against Ellie's flushed skin. For a moment, she allowed it to work its magic. She couldn't trust herself to carry on a conversation that didn't sound as if she was being pursued by stampeding horses and gasping for air.

"Where did you learn how to dance like that?" she finally managed to ask him.

Neil debated giving her a flippant, witty, noncommittal answer. But Ellie didn't strike him as the kind of woman he could just lie to or make up something for, just for the sake of sounding clever. That had never been his thing anyway.

So he told her the truth, even though it painted him in less than a flattering light.

"There was this girl in high school I was trying to impress. Rhonda. She took my breath away every time I looked at her. Someone told me that she liked to dance, so I got my mother to get me lessons."

Instantly, Neil became more human to her. Ellie could even see him in her mind's eye, pining after an unattainable girl. "And did you impress this girl?"

"No. She never even looked my way. When I asked her to go to the dance, she looked at me as if I was crazy. That's when I found out she was going with the captain of the football team. The guy had shoulders out to here," he told Ellie, holding his hands as far apart as they would go to show her just how wide those shoulders were. "I swear," he said with a laugh, "you could use those suckers as a diving board."

"Well," Ellie declared with a shrug, "her loss. A heart surgeon and a fabulous dancer. If you ask me, that's a killer combination," she told him.

"And soon to be a fantastic driver," he added. "Don't forget that," Neil reminded her, amusement curving his mouth again.

Ellie felt as if his smile had nestled directly into her chest, all but weaving its magic all through her system.

"Well, let's hold off on the 'fantastic driver'

part," Ellie advised, pointing out, "You haven't quite gotten there yet."

"But I will," he said confidently. "All I need are a couple more lessons from this fabulous, sexy teacher I have—" he looked at her and the way that the moonlight danced along her skin "—and I'll be ready for the Indy 500."

They were standing some distance away from the entrance. Out here, their main source of light came from the full moon. The semidarkness only added to the vulnerability she was experiencing.

Ellie was treading on very dangerous ground right now. If she had a brain in her head, she would get herself back inside the saloon and seek the company of others.

But she didn't.

Not just yet.

Instead, her eyes met his. "'Fabulous, sexy teacher,' huh?" she repeated.

"That's right," he confirmed.

"Are you taking lessons from someone else besides me?" she asked innocently, amusement shining in her eyes.

"No," Neil answered, turning his face toward hers as he lowered his voice to just slightly louder than a whisper. "Just you."

"Then maybe you should have your eyes

checked before you start giving Miss Joan those tests tomorrow. That is, if you want to actually be able to see the results."

"There's nothing wrong with my eyes," he assured her quietly. "I see everything just fine."

His gaze slid slowly over her face, appreciatively taking in every supple inch of her body. Making each of them warm in their own way.

"Just fine," Neil repeated as if reciting the two words like a prayer.

His eyes never left her face.

Ellie could feel her heart pounding in her throat now, threatening to take away her very last fragment of air.

"Maybe this party the sheriff threw for you is a good thing," she told him breathlessly. "You obviously don't get out very much."

But Neil had a very different opinion on the matter.

"You don't have to sample every single cookie in the box to know if the one you have is extremely sweet and the best tasting one you've ever had," he told her, his voice so low that part of her thought she was imagining the words rather than actually hearing them.

If her heart began pounding any harder, it was going to create a hole in her chest and just fall out, she thought. Even in the darkness, she knew it was only a matter of seconds before he became aware of what it was doing, how hard it was beating.

And why.

She needed to save herself before it was too late.

"Maybe we should go in," she told him.

"Maybe we should," Neil agreed.

Instead of doing that, Neil slid his fingers along her cheek, tilting her head ever so slightly. And then he slowly inclined his head and his lips met hers.

Just like that, time stood still as the kiss between them blossomed and grew until it couldn't be measured in any breadth and scope.

Ellie's mind stop protesting; stopped attempting to put the brakes on. Instead she allowed herself to be wildly, breathlessly, swept away down an uncharted river she had never even imagined in her wildest dreams existed.

Rising up on her toes, she slid her arms around his neck, felt herself eagerly responding to the heat of his body. Not just responding, but finding herself wanting more.

Eagerly.

Where had this come from? And why, in heaven's name, now?

And why with a man who couldn't possibly

want to stay in this small town once his job was done—which would be very, very soon?

It just didn't make sense, Ellie silently argued. She had always been so sensible, so practical, far more levelheaded than her years. Her behavior now was totally against type.

And yet, she realized, it didn't have to make sense. Not really. It just had to *be*.

*This* had to be.

Oh, Lord, Ellie thought, she was losing her mind. All that time she had spent up in the air was unraveling her.

The worst part was, she didn't care. She wanted to grab whatever happiness she could for however long she could.

Neil had come here looking to help, to make his life mean something. Maybe he was even looking for answers… But he hadn't come looking for this, certainly not this. And he knew that he hadn't come to Forever with any plans for remaining in this tiny dot of a town outside the length of time it took to get that old woman back on her feet and in her customary fighting form. Finding love—certainly not a soulmate—or even finding "like" had never entered into the picture.

So what was he doing out here in the shadows,

with his lips pressed against hers and his pulse all but going into orbit?

This was insane. This was ridiculous.

This was—

Heaven.

Nothing but sheer, unadulterated heaven in its purest form. And he could see why someone could become addicted to it, give up everything as long as it could be assured that, in the end, *this* would be waiting for him.

He kissed Ellie harder.

For the first time in his life, he could understand the term "head over heels."

But understanding and allowing were two different things and he had to remember that he had responsibilities and obligations. And those came first, before his own indulgences, he silently insisted.

Even so, all he wanted was to get one more minute with her. Just one more...

## *Chapter Fourteen*

"Hey, Neil, you out here?" Dan called out. He had stepped outside of the saloon and was standing in front of the entrance, squinting into the darkness and trying to make out a lone, tall figure that might, in all likelihood, be his friend.

Hearing Dan, Ellie drew back, creating a small space between herself and Neil. "I think you're being paged," she told him.

Neil sighed. It was just as well, he thought. Right now, Ellie was far too tempting and part of him was worried that if he didn't rein himself in, he could easily get carried away. There was just something about this adventurous pilot that he found exceedingly attractive.

He sighed and drew back. "So it would seem," he agreed. Raising his hand, he called out to Dan. "Over here."

Dan immediately started walking toward the sound of Neil's voice. He only stopped short when he realized that Neil wasn't alone.

*Well, this is interesting*, Dan thought. "Oh, I'm sorry. Did I interrupt anything?"

Ellie thought fast and came up with a cover story that she felt saved all three of them from any embarrassment.

"Your friend wore me out with all his fancy dancing, so I came out here to catch my breath. New York training had the Doc feeling I shouldn't be out here alone, so he volunteered to come with me." And then Ellie deftly changed the subject. "Is everything okay?" she asked. Her mind immediately went to why Neil was in Forever in the first place. "It's not Miss Joan, is it?"

Dan laughed. "Only if you're referring to her being in rarer, sharper-tongued form than usual. No," he continued, glancing at his friend, "I came out here to find Neil because it was nearly time for me to give the toast."

"The toast?" Neil repeated suspiciously. In his

opinion, enough attention had been sent his way. This had to be about his patient, or at least he hoped so. "You're talking about the one for Miss Joan, right?"

"No, I was referring to the one that is intended to include both of you. Actually," Dan confessed, "I can't take credit for this. The toast is more Rick's idea than mine. And he's the one who's going to be giving it," he explained.

Neil was already shaking his head. "I think, if it's all the same to you, I'll pass."

"Funny, those are more or less the same words that Miss Joan used a few minutes ago," Dan told him. "If you ask me, you two are a match made in heaven. You think alike."

"Nobody's asking," Neil commented pointedly, frowning at the idea of being the focus of a toast.

That was the point when Ellie decided she needed to step in. "C'mon, Doc," she urged, slipping her arm through his and tugging him toward Murphy's. "You can't insult everyone by not going in and listening to them tell you how grateful they are that you came. That's what this whole thing is about, you know."

"Sure I can," Neil countered.

Her eyes met his with a silent challenge. "Then how do you expect Miss Joan to go along with everything if you, the reasonable, big-city surgeon, doesn't?"

Dan laughed, tickled by the way Ellie had managed to turn the situation around. "She's got you there, Neil," he told his stubborn friend.

Neil sighed, mentally surrendering. He found Dan's choice of words rather appropriate as he left the shadows and began to walk toward the saloon. "Yes," he agreed with a sigh that seemed to come from the very depths of his soul as he glanced in Ellie's direction, "she does."

Ellie was positive that she was reading far too much into his words than he'd ever intended, but she still couldn't shake the feeling that there was more to them than was implied strictly on the surface.

The moment the door to the saloon was opened, everyone inside turned to the three people who were entering.

Applause and cheers greeted Neil and he found himself being separated from Ellie and Dan and tugged toward the center of Murphy's. All those bodies in one place made the atmosphere feel a great deal warmer than he had anticipated.

He had been brought in and placed right next to Miss Joan.

Her hazel eyes went over him slowly, pinning him in place.

"I see they got you, too, sonny," Miss Joan said. "I would have thought someone as clever as you would have been able to make good his escape," she commented. "Maybe you're not as clever as I gave you credit for."

Miss Joan's husband sidled up to Neil. "Don't let her get to you," Harry whispered to him. "She just doesn't know how to deal with all this attention being showered on her." He smiled fondly at his wife. "You'd think she would have gotten used to it by now."

"Sure I know how to deal with it," Miss Joan contradicted. "I just walk out on it." But when she moved to do so, she found herself surrounded by well-wishers who blocked her path. Miss Joan pursed her lips in a disapproving frown. "You'd think that grown people would have better things to do with their time than drink and give aimless speeches."

"Right now," the sheriff said, coming up between the two guests of honor, "I can't think of a single one. Everybody—" Rick raised his voice to address the room "—lift your glasses high and give your heartfelt thanks to Dr. Neil Eastwood," He turned toward Neil. "Dr. Neil left his cushy Sixth

Avenue life to come out here and make sure that Miss Joan continues giving us her sharp-tongued commentary on everything we're doing wrong." He raised his glass a little higher as he declared, "We don't know what we'd do without you and we hope it's another fifty years before we have to start worrying about finding that out."

And then he positioned himself between the two and looked out into the crowd. "To Dr. Neil and Miss Joan!" the sheriff declared.

Anything else he might have said was drowned out as a resounding chant of "To Dr. Neil and Miss Joan!" was loudly declared at just the right intervals to sound like an uncoordinated cacophony of high and low voices, some melodious, some shrilled, none of them blending harmoniously.

The only thing they all had in common was the love that was woven through them.

The party went on for more than another two hours. The time was filled with good conversation, good food and just enough drink to make it all go down easily.

The sheriff, who had helmed the entire event from start to finish, was there to help when it came time to close the party down, as well. Rick was there predominantly because he didn't want to take

any chances that either party would be too inebri-
ated to oversee the various tests scheduled for the
next morning or too unable to take said tests in the
first place. What he was looking to prevent was a
problem with the readings.

Rick was afraid that if Miss Joan became in-
toxicated, the true readings that would be necessary to make an accurate determination wouldn't
be able to be taken.

"Well, I guess I should thank you for this," Miss
Joan muttered. Her eyes swept over the sheriff as
well as two of the three Murphy brothers, Matt and
Liam, as she and her husband had begun to make
their way slowly over to the door.

Rick waved away her thanks. "There's no need,"
he told her.

Miss Joan eyed him with an annoyed air. "Well,
you boys might have been raised in a barn, but me,
I was raised with old-fashioned manners. You always say 'thank you' to the person who went out
of their way for you—even if you didn't want them
to in the first place," the woman added pointedly.

Rick smiled. "And we call *that* a backhanded
compliment," he commented to his sister, Ramona.

"You're free to call it anything you want," Miss
Joan informed him.

Placing his still powerful hands on Miss Joan's

shoulders, Harry tactfully ushered her toward the door. "I'd better get her home before she stops being so humble and nice."

"Watch your step, Old Man, or you're sleeping out in the henhouse tonight," Miss Joan warned. "With the chickens."

Unfazed, Harry merely laughed. He'd heard it all before. "That's the price I pay for wanting fresh eggs in the morning," he told Neil with a wink as he and Miss Joan left the premises.

Ellie couldn't help the grin that came to her lips. "I'll bet you don't have anything like that back where you are."

"No, we do not," Neil agreed. He'd had a really good time tonight. Far better than he would have ever expected. "I'd better call it a night myself," he told Ellie, although it was obvious to anyone paying attention that the surgeon was really reluctant to go.

"We should be going, too," Dan agreed. He had one arm around Tina as he gently ushered his wife and children before him in the general direction of the entrance. "Big day tomorrow." Slanting a glance at Neil, he added with a kindly grin, "No pressure intended."

"Right," Neil laughed. Like that changed anything. "None felt."

"So, is the appointment for the tests still set for tomorrow at 9:00 a.m.?" Ellie asked, looking from Neil to Dan.

"We figured that would be a good time so that Miss Joan doesn't decide to get a head start flying the coop," Dan told Ellie. Neil nodded his agreement.

Ellie quickly reviewed her schedule in her head. She didn't have anything for the morning and, even if she had, she knew it would be a simple enough matter to reroute a pickup flight to a later time.

She smiled to herself. That was what made currently being the only air service in town, however small it was, such a good thing.

"Need a cheering section?" she asked, looking from one doctor to the other.

It appeared that Ellie and Neil had taken to one another and Dan, for one, was quite happy about the idea.

"Sure," Dan said, answering for his friend, and then specifying, "A quiet cheering section."

"Never intended anything else," Ellie assured Dan. She turned toward Neil, not wanting to horn in unless he gave his permission, as well. "How about you?"

"How about me what?" he asked, thinking he might have lost the thread of the conversation.

"Do you have any objections to my hanging around the medical clinic tomorrow while you run your tests on Miss Joan?"

"Objections?" Neil echoed with a dry laugh. "Hell, no. We might even need you to hold her down," he said. "There's a likely possibility that Miss Joan might change her mind about being so 'agreeable' by morning when the chips are finally down."

Dan's wife, Tina, had a different take on the situation. She had known Miss Joan longer than Dan had. "I think that if Miss Joan was going to disagree about anything," she said, speaking up, "it'll be about having a procedure done at all if those tests actually point to her needing surgery."

Dan nodded. "Right, as usual, my love," he said. But rehashing all this now was moot. They needed to wait until tomorrow, "Okay, let's get these sleepyheads into bed," he said to Tina.

With that, he bent down and picked up Jeannie. The little girl looked more than happy to rest her head on her father's shoulder. She was asleep before he even managed to take two steps.

"I can remember doing that with your sister," Eduardo whispered to Ellie as he and Addie walked by, on their way out. After meeting Neil,

Addie had decided the doctor was more suited to her sister than to her and had quietly stepped back.

"Not with her?" Neil asked, looking at Ellie.

"Ellie?" Eduardo repeated incredulously as he laughed at the suggestion. "You are kidding, of course, yes? This one," he told the cardiologist, nodding at his older granddaughter, "was much too independent to ever let on that she was too tired to walk. She would have continued walking home until she fell on her knees in an exhausted heap."

"Your memory is going, Pop," Ellie told him, trying to look stern, but the affectionate laugh gave her away.

Not playing along, Eduardo shook his head. "My memory is as sharp and clear as it was on the day you came into my life."

Neil would have enjoyed staying around these people and listening to their stories until well into dawn, but he needed a clear head for the morning and that required sleep. It wasn't just that the woman he would be working on was so important—as far as he was concerned, every patient he dealt with was equally important... It was just that so many eyes would be trained on him, figuratively rather than literally, and he didn't want to even remotely run the risk of something, however minor or unintended, going wrong.

As he had already told himself, every patient was important, but Miss Joan was especially important, which was why he had to be at his best. Neil couldn't afford to just phone this in—not that he ever would—but this time he had to be even more vigilant than usual.

Belatedly, he focused on the present and announced, "I'll walk you all to your car." His words were intended not just for Ellie but for her family, as well.

Ellie answered first. "You don't have to," she told him. "I know where my Jeep is and so does Pop—and Addie," she added belatedly when her sister gave her an annoyed look at the accidental exclusion.

"Old habits die hard, remember?" Neil asked her, reminding her of what he'd said when she had pointed this out the other day.

"Let him do what he feels is right, Ellie," Eduardo gently prodded. "Nothing wrong with good manners."

"I wasn't inferring that there was, Pop," she told her grandfather, further pointing out, "Just that he needs his rest, so he is free to skip this part of his ritual."

"Now who's acting like an overprotective

mother hen?" Addie asked her sister with a knowing smirk.

Pop came close to telling Addie, "Leave your sister alone," but he managed to bite it back at the last minute, aware that neither granddaughter would appreciate the comment for different reasons.

So instead, he paused to shake Neil's hand. "Good luck tomorrow and remember Miss Joan's bark is worse than her bite."

Neil laughed. "Can I quote you on that?"

"Don't you dare," Eduardo told him with a wide, good-natured smile.

Neil merely nodded. "I didn't think so."

Miss Joan was clearly an enigma and he really wasn't a hundred percent sure just how to read her, so he decided that it was better to err on the side of caution than to just forge right in and lose the battle altogether.

## Chapter Fifteen

In hindsight, Neil would think later that day, it hadn't gone well.

He supposed that what had caused him to let his guard down in the first place was that getting Miss Joan to initially cooperate and submit to having the battery of tests had gone better than he had expected.

Once the morning arrived, however, and despite the last-minute decision to switch the venue from the clinic to Dan's cabin where he and Tina occasionally retreated when they wanted peace and quite, Miss Joan had showed up on time, accompanied by her husband, Harry. And, with an amazing minimum of grumbling, the woman had agreed to carry on with the planned testing.

The tests included an EKG, a treadmill test and, finally, an EEG—performed when Neil was dissatisfied with the results obtained from Miss Joan's treadmill test.

"Don't know why you need to make a woman my age gasp for breath because you want to have her running on a piece of moving machinery, something I'm never going to need to do in my life," Miss Joan said tersely. "But, hey, if it makes you happy, I'm willing to do it." She frowned, looking down at all the wires that Debi had attached strategically to her chest and arms for an accurate reading. "But having all these funny little electrical round things attached to places that should remain private except between a husband and his wife, creating zigzag patterns on a ticker tape while you force me to walk, just seems like a big fat waste of time," she complained.

"And as for this last one," she declared when Neil performed the EEG. "That fancy camera work to see if my heart's beating? Well…" she snorted. "You don't want to *know* my opinion of this one."

Neil merely offered her what passed for a smile as he reread the all the test readouts. He had hoped against hope that he was wrong, but it certainly didn't look that way.

*This isn't good*, he thought, raising his eyes to look at his patient.

Finished, Miss Joan had had gotten up off the gurney brought in for expressly this purpose and was buttoning up her blouse, glad to be putting it all behind her.

"But at least everyone and his brother," she was saying, "is going to stop pestering me to have these damn things done." Dressed and ready to leave, she looked at Neil. "We done here?" she asked him, fully expecting a positive response.

Neil didn't answer at first. He had seen an anomaly on the treadmill readout, one he had been afraid he would see. At the very least, it indicated that Miss Joan had a blockage and needed to have an angioplasty done. In addition, because of the arterial fibrillation, an ablation, where some of the heart tissue would have to be cut away, might also be called for.

"No, Miss Joan," he finally said, not relishing what he needed to tell her, "I'm afraid that we are *not* done here."

She watched him for a moment. Something that Ellie could have sworn that looked like fear flashed through her eyes before a somber expression set in.

"Maybe you don't understand," Miss Joan stated firmly. "We're done here." With that, the woman headed for makeshift testing room's door. "You had your fun, you played doctor," she told him crisply. "Now I've got to get back to my life."

Neil raised his voice, thinking that would stop her in her tracks. "Miss Joan, you have a blockage, not to mention a serious case of A-fib taking a toll on your heart. You need to have an angioplasty performed and probably an ablation, as well."

Miss Joan's expression was dark as she turned to look at Neil. "You are trying my patience, sonny. Can those things you just came up with, those fancy words, can they be done right here in Forever?"

"No, I'm afraid not," he told her. "Forever's clinic doesn't have the facility to perform those procedures," he said as kindly as he could. He wasn't used to having to justify his recommendations, or to having to baby his patients. "You'll need to go to a fully equipped hospital for that."

She raised her chin defiantly. "Well, I guess that answers that, doesn't it?" Miss Joan paused to give him a look that her husband had once said could have stopped a charging rhino dead in its tracks. "In case I haven't made myself clear," she informed him, "it's not happening." And with that she swept out of the room that contained all the equipment and into the outer one where her husband and Ellie were waiting. Ellie had wound up keeping the man company because he had struck her as being uncharacteristically nervous.

"Miss Joan!" Neil called after her.

The woman just continued walking. "Go tend to people who want to be fussed over. That's not me! We're done here," Miss Joan announced in no uncertain terms.

She whizzed by Harry and Ellie without a single glance in their direction.

Harry jumped to his feet, incredibly spry for a man his age. "Miss Joan?" he called after his wife.

Miss Joan just kept walking. "I'm finished playing games," she merely told her husband as she made her way out of the cabin, slamming the door in her wake.

Bewildered, not to mention worried and more than a little frightened for his wife, Harry looked at Neil for an explanation as to Miss Joan's behavior. "What you just found, is it bad, Doctor?"

It wasn't Neil's habit to disclose a diagnosis to anyone beyond the patient involved. But this was a case he had gone into knowing that he would undoubtedly need help managing the patient and, in doing so, rules he always adhered to would be bent and even broken. In view of that, he felt he had the right to disclose at least this much to Miss Joan's husband. A lot of people cared about this sharp-tongued woman.

"It's what we thought," he said, referring to what he had previously shared with Harry. "Your wife needs to have surgeries."

Harry took a deep breath, trying his best to brace himself. "More than one?"

Neil nodded. "I'm afraid so."

"And if Miss Joan refuses to have these surgeries performed?" Ellie asked, feeling that Harry needed to be prepared for the worst case scenario.

"She'd be literally rolling the dice as to how long she can keep going without suffering some sort of dire consequences," Neil answered, hoping that would give the man the ammunition he needed to make his wife realize she was being recklessly foolish.

Harry sighed haplessly. "I'll work on her," he told the doctor. "But you have to understand that she is one stubborn old woman. I know from experience that nobody is going to make Miss Joan do anything she doesn't want to do."

His shoulders slumped in what amounted to a parenthesis; he looked like a man who felt he was facing a losing battle.

"Thanks for everything, Dr. Eastwood. You did your best," he told Neil as he left the cabin to try to catch up to his wife.

Neil shook his head, totally mystified. He didn't like things that didn't make any sense. "It's not as if we don't have the technology to help her," he said to Ellie, clearly frustrated. "We do. We can."

"We'll work on her," Ellie told him, moved by how deeply affected he seemed by Miss Joan's behavior. "And by 'we,' I mean everyone in town. We'll get Miss Joan to come around."

He eyed her skeptically. After the performance he had just witnessed, he doubted it could be done. "You actually believe that?"

"We have to," she told him simply. And then Ellie glanced at her watch. Talk about bad timing. "I've got a delivery to make."

"Go," Neil told her, waving her on her way.

But Ellie noticed that the surgeon was making no effort to leave with her. She couldn't very well tell him to leave the cabin, but she didn't like the idea of his hanging back.

"You'll be all right?" she asked, concerned.

"Always have been," he replied in a distant voice.

With that, Neil turned his attention to the equipment brought into the cabin. He needed to get it ready for transport when the van's driver arrived. The guy had to take it back to the physician who had temporarily loaned the equipment to him.

Ellie hesitated. He couldn't do all this alone, she thought. "Look, I can stay awhile and help you. I'll just make a call and postpone the delivery run—"

"No," Neil said, stopping her before she could continue. "You take care of your business. I'd rather be alone right now, anyway," Neil told her.

Ellie was surprised at the extent that his words stung, but she did understand how he felt. Given his position and the breadth of his knowledge, she was sure that Neil was accustomed to having people obey his recommendations without question. He was not accustomed to being ignored like this.

This was a whole new world for him, she thought as she quietly left him to pack everything up and, more importantly, to sort out his feelings about what had just taken place.

The delivery run took her longer than Ellie had anticipated. After she was back, there were chores at the ranch she needed to catch up on. She knew that her grandfather wouldn't say anything, but she felt guilty about not doing her share.

It was after seven before she had time to turn her attention back to Neil. She hoped he had come to terms with today's events and had had found a way to deal with them. This wasn't over by a long shot, even though it might have felt that way to him.

Ellie stopped by the medical clinic, thinking she would find him there with Dan even though it was technically about to close down for the night.

She was disappointed.

"Haven't seen him in the last couple of hours," Dan told her as he saw his last patient of the day to the door. "After Neil packed up all the equipment he'd borrowed to do Miss Joan's tests and it was picked up, he said he had somewhere to be. He told me that he'd be by my place later on tonight, possibly a lot later." Dan looked at Ellie with compassion. "I think this thing with Miss Joan hit him kind of hard. He's not used to having his advice ignored," he sighed, empathizing with his friend. "He's frustrated that she won't listen to reason."

Ellie nodded. "It's a large club."

"I know, right? But Neil's a grown man and he'll work this out for himself," he assured Ellie and then confessed, "I just hate having put him in this position. I really thought she might listen to reason once she agreed to being examined." Dan began closing up, thinking this was early for him.

"I'll let Neil know you were looking for him once he turns up," he promised.

Ellie nodded as she left the clinic. But she wasn't patient enough just to sit around, waiting for Neil just to turn up. He'd looked really upset and she wanted to comfort him.

The man had to be somewhere, she reasoned.

Ellie swung by Murphy's, thinking he might want to get an anonymous drink to kill some time.

But he wasn't there.

She took a quick look into the diner, thinking that maybe he had decided to give talking Miss Joan into having the surgeries one more try.

But he wasn't at the diner, either.

She left before Miss Joan saw her, not ready to confront the woman just yet.

*Okay, so where was he?*

Ellie doubted that he would go wandering around the countryside, not without having a destination in mind. As far as she knew, there was only one place left to try before she gave up her search.

Operating on instinct, Ellie swung by the ranch house to pick up a few things from the refrigerator and the pantry, and to pack them into an old basket that she and her sister used to use for picnics. Mentally crossing her fingers, Ellie drove back to Dan's cabin. It was the only place she could think of where Neil might feel comfortable enough to just hang around while he tried to figure out what to do about Miss Joan.

Approaching, Ellie saw one lone light in the window and knew she had guessed right.

Parking her Jeep, she took the picnic basket with her and presented herself at the front door. She knocked. There was no response, so she knocked again. And then a third time.

"I'm not going to go away, Doc," she announced, about to knock for a fourth time.

That was when the door finally opened. Neil stood in the doorway, his body prohibiting entrance. Looking at her, he shook his head. "You people are a really persistent bunch, aren't you?"

"You're just picking up on that?" she asked with a grin. Raising the basket she was holding to get his attention, she said, "I figured you hadn't eaten anything yet and Dr. Dan wouldn't want you starving while you were his guest, so I brought food."

Neil eyed the basket, making no effort to take it. "Is that from Miss Joan's Diner?"

"No," she told him. "It's from my kitchen. I figured you wouldn't eat anything that came from her diner right now and the bottom line here is that I really want you to eat."

Neil frowned and then stepped back, allowing

her to enter. He shut the door behind her. "Why would that matter to you?"

"Ouch," she cried, dramatically placing her hand over her heart. "That's kind of cold," Ellie told him. "You really have to ask?"

Neil sighed. He wasn't behaving like himself, he silently admonished. "Sorry. This thing with Miss Joan has really set me off."

"The way she's behaving is nothing personal against you," Ellie insisted.

Coming into the outer room, she set her basket down and proceeded to take out what she'd packed, which included some pieces of fried chicken, side dishes of potato salad and carrots, as well as something to drink, plates, utensils, napkins and two glasses. She set them all on a makeshift table. "Like most of us, Miss Joan doesn't like facing her own mortality. Her thinking is if she doesn't admit there's something wrong, then whatever is wrong can't kill her."

"Except that it can," he said. "Miss Joan is too smart a woman not to know that," he insisted.

"She does know that," Ellie assured him. "But give her time. She needs to work this through at her own pace," she told Neil. "Meanwhile, everyone is working on her to make her realize that having this operation is the lesser of two evils—

the bigger evil in this case being dying," she concluded flatly.

"Now, you do your part and eat, Doc, or when we finally *do* get through to that stubborn woman, you might not be up to doing what actually needs to be done," she told him.

He looked at the food she had put on the table. "I'm not hungry."

She wasn't buying it. "The hell you're not. By my calculation, you haven't eaten since early this morning. By now, you should be ready to chew on cardboard. Sit," she ordered, pointing to one of the chairs at the table. "Eat."

He looked at her as if he couldn't believe what he was hearing. "I—"

"Don't talk," Ellie cut in. "Eat. Now," she told him.

Because the whole scenario struck him as almost ludicrous, Neil found himself grinning at Ellie in response.

"Yes, ma'am."

Ellie nodded, pleased. "Better. Just so you know, you can't be engaging in a battle of wills with Miss Joan. Trust me, you'll be a casualty in that war. The woman has had years of practice at it and she'll win, hands down."

He saw no point in arguing with that. She was

probably right. "I can't believe how someone who knows that there are all these people around who care about her the way they do can willfully disregard her health like this."

Ellie waved her hand at his statement. "Oh, believe it," she told him. "We all told you how stubborn that woman can be," she reminded him.

"I know, but…" he sighed.

Without thinking, he picked up a piece of fried chicken and took a bite of it. The moment he started chewing, he looked up at Ellie, traces of surprise on his face.

"Hey, this is good," he told her. "You made this?"

"Yes. You sound surprised," she observed.

"It's just that…well, you've got all these other things that you're good at, like flying a plane. I didn't think you'd be good at doing domestic things, too," he confessed.

"You mean like cooking," she guessed with a smile. "Or, by 'domestic things,' are you referring to making beds and doing laundry?"

He knew when he'd made a mistake. "I'm tripping over my own tongue."

"That's okay," Ellie said. She thought of when Neil had kissed her and felt a warm shiver undulate down her spine. "It's rather a nice tongue, so you're forgiven."

He laughed. "You have a way with words," he told her. "I guess there's nothing you can't do when you set your mind to it."

Ellie cocked her head, looking at him, bemused. "Is that a challenge?"

"I don't know," Neil replied honestly. "It might be." His eyes met hers. "Do you want it to be?"

She could feel her heart actually skip a beat as her skin heated so quickly it took her very breath away. She was acutely aware of the fact that the ball had just been lobed into her court and it was up to her to either let it fall at her feet or to return it.

Ellie more than happily returned the serve.

## Chapter Sixteen

Getting up from her seat, Ellie came around to Neil's side of the table.

She wove her arms around his neck and said, "Yes," in a low, breathy whisper just before she brought her mouth down to his and kissed him.

By turns surprised and then exceedingly pleased, Neil pushed his chair away from the table and pulled Ellie onto his lap. He managed all this while never removing his lips from hers.

The kiss deepened.

It continued to grow in intensity, making Ellie's head spin so much, she felt as if she had lost her bearings, not to mention any grip on reality.

For a second, she couldn't even remember where she was.

All she was aware of was Neil, who was setting her whole body on fire.

Neil kissed her over and over again, making the entire world fade away until it was nothing more than a pinprick in the scope of the universe.

Yes, he had kissed her before and it had been a really, really wonderful experience. But this was on an entirely different level.

This was something spectacular and oh, so hot. Her pulse was beating so hard, the rhythm reverberated throughout.

Though her breath was growing shorter and shorter, Ellie didn't want to break away and come up for air. She definitely didn't want what she was experiencing to stop.

She closed her arms around Neil's neck, huddling her body closer to his, glorying in the warmth transferring from his body to hers.

Neil was aware that he was pressing his advantage and a sense of propriety was telling him that he really should be putting the brakes on before this went too far—if it hadn't already.

Maybe it was his state of mind, but he just couldn't help himself, couldn't keep from absorbing and glorying in everything that this woman had to offer.

Her sweetness. Her sustenance. The delicious ripeness of her mouth pressed against his.

Oh, Lord, her wonderful mouth.

He couldn't get enough of her, feasting on everything Ellie had to offer and craving more.

Even so, Neil forced himself to pull back. As wonderful as this was—and this *was* wonderful— he felt he wasn't allowing her to think, much less to say no if she was so inclined. Neil didn't want to overwhelm her, he wanted her to want him of her own free volition.

Drawing his head back, he asked her, "Do you want me to stop?"

Ellie stared at him, bewildered. She couldn't understand why Neil would ask her that. "Why? Did I do something wrong?"

"You?" he questioned, stunned. The woman had to be the closest thing to perfect he had ever encountered. "Lord, no. I just didn't want to railroad you into doing something you might not want to do."

She didn't think she could be so touched while lost in the wild throes of overwhelming desire, but she was. He was being gallant. More than that, he was actually willing to step away if she didn't want this to happen—which just made her want it all the more.

Ellie could feel herself growing very, very warm as passion swept through her.

She framed his face with her hands, already making love with him in her mind, and warned, "You just try to stop now and see what happens."

Neil grinned then, his heart swelling. The emptiness he had been harboring began to evaporate. This was, he couldn't help thinking, exactly what he needed both to help him cope with the events that had transpired this morning as well as to finally come to terms with what had gone down between him and Judith. He had been right to end his soul-draining engagement and now he could see why. Because it left him open to the promise that Ellie bore within her.

She was his destiny even though he hadn't seen it at the time. It was both unnerving and exhilarating.

"You're a scary lady, Ellie Montenegro," Neil told her.

Her eyes were filled with laughter as she replied, "You have no idea, Dr. Eastwood."

"Okay," he declared. "Enough of this chitchat. More kissing."

And with that, Neil kissed her again, harder and

with even more enthusiasm than he had displayed the last time.

Her head began spinning again. All the available oxygen was being sucked out, leaving her caught up in a world filled with only him. A sensation she desperately wanted to continue.

By degrees, Ellie became aware that he was picking her up, aware that he was carrying her to the other room while her mouth remained sealed to his, affording her the very sustenance she needed to thrive.

When Neil finally drew his lips away from hers, she almost felt bereft. But then that feeling faded as he began to trace his lips along her neck, her throat, the planes of her face. Anointing all of her and making her desperately eager for more.

Ellie gave back as good as she got. For every place along her body that Neil kissed, she returned the favor. She was almost desperate to devour him with her eager mouth, wanting to do to him what he was so clearly doing to her.

She was acutely aware of the fact that when it came right down to it, she hardly knew Neil, but that didn't really matter. Her *soul* knew him, *had* known him, she felt.

It made no sense in reality—wouldn't have made any sense to her had someone said this to her only a short while ago. And yet, in her heart, she knew that what she felt was true.

And if what was happening between them never went anywhere beyond tonight, she would deal with that later. Right now, the only thing that mattered was this moment, this man. This wondrous feeling that was exploding within her and creating incredible rainbows in her soul.

Ellie gloried in his artful hands, which touched her everywhere, caressing her, possessing her, making her feel incredibly beautiful, cherished and wanted.

Her heart pounding, she was only vaguely aware of unbuttoning Neil's shirt, pushing it away from his wide shoulders and down his arms. She was eager to feel his naked body beneath the material. Eager to touch and caress. And possess him.

She could feel him doing the very same thing to her as she undid his trousers, tugging them away from his torso.

Ellie could hardly recognized herself.

She had never behaved this way before. But then, she had never *felt* this way before. It was as if some sort of wild animal within her had been set free, given the go-ahead to behave in a manner that was completely foreign to her.

Ellie didn't even want to think what had to be

going through Neil's mind about her right at this moment. About what he thought about her wanton behavior. All that was secondary to this moment, this sensation, this man who had lit her fire and managed to set her off this way—making her sizzle.

She wanted more. More of this fantastic sensation. More of *him*.

Neil couldn't even begin to describe what he was feeling right now. This woman with the adorable face was behaving in ways he wouldn't have ever even begun to imagine.

She took his very breath away. It was like handling liquid fire, trying desperately to contain it without getting burned, and yet being utterly fascinated by it.

Neil was creating havoc within her as he was covering her eager, throbbing body with a network of hot, openmouthed kisses. With each one, though it didn't seem possible, he only managed to fuel his desire to higher and higher levels.

He was making her crazy, Ellie thought. He was blotting out her very thoughts with what he was doing, leaving her to be a throbbing mass of pulsating, yearning desire.

Working his magic, he had managed, by using

his clever mouth, to bring her up to one climax and then quickly to another.

It was all she could do to keep from screaming out loud.

Ellie bit down on her lip, holding in her exploding joy as it seized her—but it wasn't easy.

After each episode, she fell back on the gurney, exhausted beyond her wildest imagination as well as incredibly sated.

The second time it occurred, she didn't think she would be able to even move, but at the same time, she felt guilty that she had received all the pleasure and he hadn't.

When she realized that Neil was beginning to undertake the same path again, Ellie put her hands against his shoulders and stopped him. And then, before he could say a word, she drew him up to her level.

"Together," she breathed. Her meaning was as clear as she was able to make it, given the fact that she was having trouble dragging in air.

"Whatever you want," Neil told her. There was a gleam in his eyes as he slowly dragged his body up along hers, arousing both of them as he did so.

Neil was more than ready for her, but even so, he wove a wreath of kisses all along Ellie's face and neck one more time before he finally united them and entered her.

And then he began to move. At first slowly, then faster and faster, until they found themselves racing, breathlessly, to the final pinnacle, the final all-engulfing explosion. When it came, wrapping itself around both of them, the impact was so surprisingly powerful it all but disoriented them.

They clung to one another, holding on tightly and relishing every single nuance about the moment.

Ellie felt like there were stars exploding in her head, dancing through her very system. Everything else she had ever felt before paled in comparison. She held on to him, clinging to Neil and to the moment, wishing with all her heart that it would never end.

But she knew it had to. And when it did, the sadness that drenched her was all but overwhelming.

Ellie hung on until she managed to surface from the sadness, her breathing coming in short spurts until she finally managed to steady her pulse, getting it down to a normal rate.

Neil's arm tightened around her, holding her close to him. The feel of his heart beating against hers was incredibly comforting, more than she had ever thought possible.

Ellie sealed the moment to her, preserving it so that she could remember this in the times when Neil would no longer be there with her.

"Well, I have to admit that I never saw the day ending like this," Neil said, lightly kissing the top of her head.

"Is that a good thing or a bad thing?" Ellie asked him.

"It's an unusual thing," he answered because although, quite honestly, he had wanted to make love to Ellie practically from the first moment he had first laid eyes on her, he hadn't really thought he would wind up doing it. He had felt that Ellie seemed to be out of his reach.

"Oh," she replied, thinking that perhaps he was already putting distance between them.

He thought he could detect a note of disappointment in her voice and he certainly hadn't intended to offend her in any way.

"But it's definitely a good thing," he told her with a broad smile. "A very good thing," he stressed. "In fact, it's so good that I'm thinking of getting my strength up for seconds," he teased.

"You need to get your strength up?" she asked.

He struck her as being such a hearty, robust specimen of virile manhood.

"Hey, don't kid yourself, fly-girl," he told her with a straight face. "You took a hell of a lot out of me just now."

She was trying to follow him. If he was drained, why did he want to go another round? "But you want to go again?"

"Oh, I definitely want to go again," Neil said with enthusiasm.

"Mmm," she murmured, turning her nude body into his. "So just how long do you think you'll need to get your strength back up?"

He pretend to think. "Hard to say," he answered, his voice trailing off.

Ellie began to kiss him, at first with small, butterfly kisses then she progressed to longer, deeper ones that crisscrossed his face and torso, anointing every part of him.

"Is it getting any easier to say?" she asked Neil as she went on kissing him.

"Not yet," he answered, his voice catching. Then he changed that answer to, "Well, maybe just a little easier." And then that changed to, "I think it might be soon. Very, very soon," he amended, as she continued kissing his face and throat, then worked her way—slowly—down along his chest, moving ever lower.

Ellie could feel his heart pounding beneath her parted lips.

"In my humble opinion," she told Neil, "I think you're going to be ready for round two…oh, just about any minute now."

As she said it, she feathered her fingers along his nether regions, mischief in her eyes as she grinned wickedly. She could feel his response to her growing as she stroked.

He caught her hand before she could continue. Ellie was really making him crazy, he thought, wanting her more with every passing second.

"You keep doing that, Ellie, and I'm not going to be responsible for whatever consequences are going arise," he told her.

She pretended to think it over and her wicked smile grew wider. "I think I'll take my chances," she told him with a laugh.

Catching her up in his arms, Neil rolled over onto her.

"Round two," he announced, his eyes shining as he went on to make love to her.

Ellie didn't waste her time with a verbal response. In her opinion, actions spoke louder.

Much louder, and their time together was growing shorter and shorter.

She fought off and blocked the pang that threatened to seize her.

Everything had grown so complicated but she couldn't think of that now.

She just wanted to make love with Neil now. She would think about all the rest later.

Much later.

## Chapter Seventeen

"You're getting in kind of late, aren't you?" Eduardo commented when Ellie drove up to the ranch house in her Jeep and got out.

Her grandfather was sitting on the front porch in the weathered rocking chair that he had once carved for his daughter-in-law when she was first pregnant with Ellie. It was close to midnight and she had thought that Pop would have been in bed by now.

"I was getting a little concerned," he went on to tell her.

She came up the porch steps and stopped at his chair. "Pop, I'm a big girl now," she reminded him affectionately. "You don't have to worry about me."

"Doesn't matter how 'big' you are or how old you are," he told her matter-of-factly. "I'm always going to worry about you and your sister. It's what family does," he said simply. "So, is everything all right?" Eduardo asked.

He wasn't the type to pry. Ellie was right, she was past the age where he felt he needed to be overly protective of her and keep track of what she did. But at the same time, he was determined to always be there for his granddaughters should they ever feel that they needed him.

She decided that since he had waited up, he deserved to hear part of the story. "Dr. Eastwood finally got to run those tests on Miss Joan."

Eduardo nodded. He'd hoped that Miss Joan would live up to her word. "So how did that go?"

Ellie sighed. "Not well," she confessed. "The test results showed that she needs to have surgery and she didn't want to hear about it. Dr. Eastwood isn't used to being disregarded and I think her reaction really bothered him. I tried to make him feel better about the situation by telling him that it wasn't him, it was just Miss Joan being Miss Joan," she told her grandfather.

If he suspected that anything else happened beyond that, she knew he wasn't going to push the matter. It was an unspoken agreement between them.

"Well," Eduardo said thoughtfully, "he knew that going in."

"Yes," she agreed, "but knowing something and being confronted with it are two very different things. It hit him hard. He felt he should have been able to convince her to have the procedure."

"So, were you able to make the good doctor come around and feel better?" Eduardo asked.

It was hard to keep the smile from her face, but she didn't want to have to explain about that, too, so all she said was, "I think so."

Eduardo's eyes met hers. She could see that she hadn't completely convinced him, but he wasn't about to push the matter.

"Good," he pronounced. "Get some sleep, Ellie. Maybe things will look better by tomorrow."

That had always been her grandfather's guiding mantra, she thought. "Maybe," she echoed. "G'night, Pop."

He rose slowly from the rocking chair, his limbs not as cooperative as they used to be.

"Hold on, I'm going to call it a night, too," he said, walking into the house with her.

Ellie's cell phone rang early the next morning. She was groping around for the device she'd left on her nightstand before she was fully awake.

Finding it, she held it up to her ear. "Hello?" she mumbled thickly.

"I found her!"

The woman's excited voice echoed in Ellie's head before she could make any sense of the declaration or discern who the caller was.

"Found who?" she asked, sitting up as she dragged one hand through her hair, desperately trying to bring consciousness to her brain along with it.

"Zelda. I found Zelda," the woman on the other end cried. And then, in case Ellie was still only half-awake, she added, "Miss Joan's sister. She's alive!"

Ellie blinked as she realized who was calling her—and why. "Olivia?"

"Of course it's me. Who did you think it was?" The lawyer didn't wait for an answer as she continued with her effusive narrative. "I located Miss Joan's sister," she repeated. "I had a long talk with her, told her what was going on with Miss Joan, and she's more than willing to come out and talk to her sister. She is concerned, though, that Miss Joan might not want to talk to her."

The full import of what Olivia was telling her was taking root.

"Don't worry about that part. I'll take care of

it," Ellie told the lawyer. "You did the hard part. You found her," Ellie declared. "How *did* you manage to find her?"

"Networking," Olivia answered glibly. "By the way, I heard about Miss Joan's reaction to the test results yesterday."

Ellie suspected that by now probably half the town, if not more, had heard about Miss Joan's stubborn refusal to have anything done to alleviate her condition. But now that Olivia had been able to actually find the woman's sister, this gave them a measure of hope that they would be able to get Miss Joan to come around and change her mind.

She was aware that this was a long shot, but at least now there was one.

"I'm sending Cash out to bring her back to Forever," Olivia was saying. "Any way you look at it, this is going to prove to be very interesting," the sheriff's wife told Ellie.

Ellie couldn't help but laugh. "You do have a way of understating things, Olivia. Well, I'd better get up and get dressed. Eastwood is going to want to be there for this auspicious reunion. And who knows, maybe this really will get Miss Joan to finally come around."

"One can only hope," Olivia replied wistfully.

\* \* \*

Ellie never dawdled in the morning, not even when she was a little girl getting ready for school. She had always been too conscientious. However, this had to be the fastest that she had ever gotten ready in her life. Less than ten minutes after she had received the phone call from Olivia, she was up, dressed and out the door with a piece of toast in her hand.

Eduardo had just come down the stairs when Ellie hurried past him to get out the front door.

"Hey, where's the fire?" he asked.

She didn't want to stop, but she did. She wasn't in the habit of ignoring her grandfather.

"Olivia found Miss Joan's sister. Cash is being sent out to bring her into town and I just wanted to tell Neil the good news that all isn't lost."

"Oh, so it's Neil now, is it?" Eduardo murmured to himself with a knowing smile. "Interesting," he commented, nodding his head as he went into the kitchen. "Very interesting."

Ellie lost no time driving to the Davenport residence in town. She knew for a fact that Dan was always up early because he needed to get to the medical clinic and open it for business. It had been that way ever since he had first arrived in Forever and reopened the clinic. Ellie also knew that with three children, Tina was perforce an early riser, as well.

She had no idea what Neil was accustomed to doing, but she knew he'd welcome this news and would want to hear it as soon as possible.

Ellie only needed to ring the doorbell once and the door flew open.

Tina's youngest was standing in the doorway. The moment Jeannie saw who it was, an amazingly sympathetic look came over her small face as she asked, "Are you sick, Ellie? Do you need to come in and see my dad?" The girl obviously associated anyone who came to their house with being a potential patient of her father.

"No, honey. I'm just here to give your dad and his houseguest, Dr. Eastwood, some really good news," Ellie told the little girl.

"What news is that?" Neil asked, coming into the living room and joining Jeannie and Ellie.

He smiled broadly at Ellie. The events of yesterday evening were still very much on his mind and he found himself reliving them over and over again—and wanting to generate even more memories.

Assuming that Ellie might be there for that very same reason, Neil started to tell her, "You know,

I don't have anything really planned for today, so if you're interested—"

But he wasn't able to get any further than that because Ellie blurted out, "Olivia's located Miss Joan's sister. Cash is on his way now to pick her up and bring her back here."

It suddenly occurred to Ellie that she didn't even know where the woman lived or how long it was going to take Cash to get her and bring her back to Forever.

"You really do keep managing to surprise me," Neil told her with a shake of his head. He was aware of why they had been looking for the other woman and he honestly hadn't held out much hope for success, but then, he had been wrong before. "You think this long-lost sister that's been turned up can talk some sense into Miss Joan's head?"

"To be honest, I have no idea," Ellie admitted as Jeannie stood in the room, taking everything in, happy to be there with the adults. "But it's worth a try. I think finding Zelda—"

"Hold it. Her name is Zelda?" Neil questioned incredulously. "You mean like in that game?"

Ellie was aware of the fact that the name was not exactly a common one anymore and that the mention of it tended to bring up images of a video game, but that couldn't be helped.

"Everyone's got to be called something," she told him with a shrug. "The important thing is that she's on her way here and she might be able to get Miss Joan to listen to reason."

Neil had his doubts. "What makes you think Miss Joan will listen to her any more than she'd listen to anyone else?" he asked.

"Hope," Ellie answered simply.

He hadn't been here all that long and already he'd known that was going to be her response. "Ah, that old chestnut," he said, nodding. He wasn't trying to belittle her belief, he just didn't put as much stock in hope as Ellie did.

Ellie shrugged, dismissing his attitude. "Better than nothing."

"That's true," he said. "Okay, let's hope that your old-fashioned theories bear fruit because, frankly, the longer Miss Joan waits to have this done, the more of a risk she's running of having a fatal heart attack or something along those lines."

He wasn't saying anything that Ellie, as well as the others involved in Miss Joan's world, didn't already know.

Olivia decided that it was for the best if Dan and Neil met Zelda first before they descended on Miss Joan with her in tow.

Zelda turned out to live in a small suburb outside of Dallas. She was a tall, thin woman with a gaunt face, salt-and-pepper hair and dark eyes that looked as if they could bore right into a person's soul. There was an overwhelming sadness about her.

"Look," Zelda told the two doctors, "I appreciate what you people are trying to do, but I seriously doubt that I can talk Joan into anything. We haven't spoken to one another in over thirty years, not since—" She stopped for a moment then changed direction. "Well, not for over thirty years," Zelda repeated. She became even more solemn. "Her last words to me were 'I never want to see you again. Ever!' That's not exactly somebody who would be willingly convinced by anything I had to say."

"A lot of time has passed," Ellie reminded Miss Joan's sister. "Maybe Miss Joan is ready to forgive and forget, she just doesn't know how to go about it. Did she even know how to contact you?"

Zelda shook her head. "No, but I doubt she even tried." She was long past tears, but the solemnity she bore went deep. "I can't even blame her. What I did was pretty unforgivable."

Neil paused, scrutinizing her. He had seen that look before, on the faces of people resigned to living a life in perpetual hell for something they felt they had done, something they were guilty of.

"Let me ask you something," Neil said.

Zelda raised her chin, bracing herself. "Go ahead."

"Have you forgiven yourself?" he asked.

Zelda squared her shoulders, looking like a woman who was about to become extremely defensive. But then it was as if the air had just been let out of her. "No, I haven't."

"Don't you think it's about time that you did?" he asked. "Because, if you can't forgive yourself, then how is Miss Joan supposed to forgive you?"

Zelda shrugged, a hopeless expression on her face. "I guess that, deep down, she's not," she answered.

"That's not going to help her any," Neil told the estranged sister. "And, deep down, under all this, Miss Joan needs help. I think the fact that she does might be scaring her most of all."

Zelda sighed, mentally taking a step back. "Well, if you really believe that I can actually help, then count me in. I want to be able to help Joan in any way that I can because I can never make up for what happened."

"You need to put that behind you," Ellie told the woman. "What counts now is the present and, after that, the future. Everyone in this town cares about your sister. In her own unique, inimitable way, she has made a big difference in a lot of people's lives. They don't want anything to happen to her if it can, in any way, be prevented."

Zelda nodded. "Understood. I'm willing to do anything I can," she repeated.

Neil nodded. "All right then, let's do this," he told Zelda and the others.

The noonday rush had just concluded and activity at the diner was settling down when Ellie and Neil walked in.

Miss Joan looked up, her expression impossible to read. "I thought there was a disturbance in the atmosphere."

She still didn't look entirely friendly, as if she was holding herself in check. "If you two are hungry, take a seat. But I'm telling you that if you're here to try to talk me into letting you operate on me or alter me in any way, you're just wasting your time and your breath. I don't want to be cut open, and if that means that my time is limited, well so be it. I've made my peace with that and you should, too. Now—" she looked from one to the other "—what can I get you?"

"A better attitude," Ellie told her.

"Sorry, fresh out of that. And my attitude is my own business, missy," she informed Ellie.

"That would be fine if there's nothing to be done for you, Miss Joan, but there is and it's not even anything major," Neil insisted.

"That's a matter of opinion, sonny." She gestured toward herself. "These are all original factory parts and they're staying that way."

"I see nothing's changed. You always were as stubborn as a mule," Zelda said as she entered from the side and walked up to the counter. The woman had managed to slip in unnoticed because Miss Joan had been so focused on the two people talking to her.

Miss Joan paled the moment she heard her sister's voice. And then her eyes narrowed into small slits. "What the hell are you doing here?"

"Trying to talk some sense into you," the other woman answered. "You have people here who care about you, who are used to putting up with your abuse just because they're worried about you and want you to be well. Don't you realize how important that is? How precious? How can you even *think* about throwing all that away because you're too afraid to listen to reason and have some simple procedure done?" Zelda asked.

As the others looked on, they saw Miss Joan's face grow red as fury set in.

"Get out of here!" Miss Joan shouted at her sister, pointing to the door. "Get out of here this minute!" And when no one made a move, she all but growled, "I mean *now*!"

## Chapter Eighteen

Rather than leave, Neil took a step forward. He didn't handle this sort of stubbornness well and he was on the verge of having it out with Miss Joan. And at this point, he had nothing to lose.

Sensing what was about to happen, Ellie put her hand on his forearm, silently stopping him. When he looked at her, she slowly moved her head from side to side. This wasn't the time or the place for this sort of confrontation. Too many people were in the diner and she knew that Miss Joan wouldn't appreciate this kind of public display. They could try talking to her later, when she was relatively alone. That was their only hope of getting through to the woman.

For a couple of moments, Neil appeared to struggle with indecision but then he finally relented. He blew out a breath and, in an effort to hold on to his temper, he turned toward the door.

"Let's go," was all he trusted himself to say at the moment.

Meanwhile, Ellie hooked her arm through Zelda's and turned Miss Joan's sister around toward the door, as well. She urged the woman to leave with them.

"You know this just isn't right," Neil said heatedly as they walked out of the diner. "I never met anyone so damn bullheaded, so incredibly perverse—"

"I know," Ellie agreed. "But we can't kidnap Miss Joan and force her to have the surgery," she pointed out. She shrugged as she went down the front steps. "Who knows, maybe if we leave her alone, she'll come around on her own."

"And maybe pigs'll start flying," Neil retorted, still angry.

"Well, if I were you, I wouldn't hold my breath in either case," Zelda advised, a really sad expression on her face.

All three reached the bottom of the steps, and were about to head into the parking lot, when the diner door slammed against the opposite wall behind them.

They all turned in unison when they heard Laurel, one of the younger waitresses, plaintively cry, "Wait!" as she came running down the steps, trying to catch them before they left.

Ellie barely got the words "Why, what happened now?" out when Laurel came running up to them, looking terrified.

"It's Miss Joan!"

Neil took the steps two at a time, reaching the diner door in the blink of an eye.

"What happened?" he asked, repeating Ellie's question as he, Ellie and Zelda poured back into the diner.

Laurel was right behind them. "Miss Joan just grabbed her chest and keeled over. She didn't even say a word, she just went down," she cried breathlessly. Grabbing Neil's arm, she was in a state of panic as she looked at him with wide, frightened eyes. "She's not—not—not—"

The young woman couldn't bring herself to even frame the question.

The other waitress on duty, Vanessa, was kneeling on the floor beside Miss Joan's still body, holding her hand and desperately trying to bring the older woman around.

"I think I found a pulse," Vanessa told Neil as he knelt next to her.

Relieved to have the doctor back, the young woman scrambled to her feet to give him room.

The diner owner was on the floor, looking so incredibly pale, she had everyone thinking the worst had transpired.

All eyes were on Neil. No one spoke, no one even dared breathe, as he quickly examined Miss Joan, taking in her vital signs and trying to assess her condition.

Unable to keep silent any longer, Zelda finally demanded, "How is she?"

The expression on Neil's face was grim as he looked at Miss Joan's sister and then at Ellie. "It's not good," he answered. "I need to get her to a hospital as fast as possible."

"The closest hospital to Forever is over fifty miles away," Angel told him. Like everyone else at the diner, Miss Joan's cook had ventured out from where she was working and gathered around the fallen woman.

"You go fast, the ride there will kill her," Ed Hale, one of the many regulars at the diner, predicted.

"Yeah, but if he drives slow, she might die on the way," Allison Farrow argued.

"I can fly her there," Ellie told Neil. Her mind racing, she made a mental note of everything that needed to be done. "Someone get Harry," she ordered as she headed for the door. "He needs to know about this. Angel, you call Cash," she told the woman. "Tell him what happened." The last person she looked at was Neil. "I'll be right back," she promised. And then she raised her voice. "I need everyone to clear their cars out the parking lot. I'm going to have to land my plane there," she told the people in the diner just before she raced out of the front door.

Zelda suddenly came to life. The diner's patrons were all looking at one another, their concern all but paralyzing them. No one was making a move to get to their vehicles.

"You heard her," Zelda said in a voice that could have easily been mistaken for Miss Joan's. "Get those cars out of the way right now! She's gonna need to land her plane." Turning to Neil, Miss Joan's sister asked, "What can I do?"

Neil was working over Miss Joan, trying to make sure that her heart was not going to stop again. He didn't want to press his luck.

He barely glanced at Zelda, afraid to look away from the pale woman on the floor.

"I think you already did it," he told the woman.

Zelda knelt beside her sister and took hold of her hand, squeezing it as tightly as she dared. Her eyes began to fill.

"Damn you, old woman. You can't die before you forgive me, you hear me? Don't you dare die on me!" she ordered, tears sliding down her thin cheeks.

One of the diner's patrons had gone to the medical clinic to get Dan. The latter all but burst in through the door.

"What happened?" he cried as he knelt on the floor beside Neil in front of Miss Joan.

"She had another attack," Neil said, summing it up simply. "This one was a lot stronger than the last one. There's no way to avoid it, she's going to need an operation," he told Dan. "Ellie went to get her plane. In all likelihood, we're fighting against the clock. We're going to have to fly Miss Joan to the hospital."

And then, since he was relatively unfamiliar with the hospitals around that region, Neil asked, "What's the name of the best hospital in close proximity?"

Dan didn't even have to think. "That would be Lincoln Memorial. They've got a great cardiology department. I know one of the doctors there," Dan added.

"I think you'd better call them," Neil told him, never taking his eyes off Miss Joan. The woman was barely holding on. "Tell them we're bringing them a cardiac patient and we're going to need to use one of their operating rooms stat."

Harry came in at that moment. He was clearly terrified when he saw his wife on the floor of the diner.

"Can you save her?" he asked Neil, his voice trembling as he bravely fought not to break down. He knew he needed to remain stoic for Miss Joan's sake.

"I damn well am going to try," Neil answered, momentarily looking up and exchanging glances with Dan. "I'm going to need you to come with me," he told Dan. He felt that if they were both there, accompanying the woman to the hospital, Miss Joan had more of a fighting chance to survive than if only he was with her on the flight, even though it was going to be a short one and he was bringing an oxygen tank and a defibrillator with him.

Dan offered the other doctor an encouraging smile. "That goes without saying, Neil."

"I have to come, too," Harry told them, speaking up. "I'm her next of kin." The phrase all but stuck in his throat and he nearly broke down as he'd said it, but he managed to push on. "I have to be there to give my permission so you can do whatever you have to do to save this cantanker-ous woman who is the love of my life. It took me years to convince her to marry me. I can't lose her now." Unable to hold it together any longer, Harry quietly began to sob as he struggled to get himself back under control.

"I'm coming, too," Zelda declared as she came back into the diner and picked up the thread of the conversation. "No way she's going anywhere with-out me," she informed the doctors. "By the way, the parking lot's clear."

Hearing Zelda's statement about coming with them, Neil looked as if he had his doubts. "How many people can Ellie's plane hold?"

"Six," Ellie answered as she quickly crossed the diner floor back to Neil and Dan. "It can hold six." She immediately looked at Miss Joan. She had never seen the woman look so ashen. "How is she doing?" she whispered, as if afraid that anything louder might affect Miss Joan in an adverse way.

"Better once we get her to the hospital," Neil answered. "You know how to get to Lincoln Me-morial?" he asked, not wanting to take anything for granted at this point.

"I know how to get to anywhere in this state,"

Ellie assured him. Ready to go, she looked around. "Do you have something you can use as a gurney for her?"

Neil shook his head. "We don't have time to look for anything." He made a judgment call. "I'm going to carry her. She doesn't weigh that much."

But Dan moved in. "It's better if I take her feet and you take the upper torso. Once we have her off the ground, *then* you can carry her," he told his friend, adding, "No offense, but we don't want to risk the chance of dropping her."

Neil opened his mouth to argue that, if anything, the woman was a lightweight, but he knew that Dan was right. He didn't want to take any chances.

Meanwhile, as the two physicians sorted out just how to carry Miss Joan to the plane, Ellie dashed out of the diner and hurried back to her plane. Opening the doors, she waited as Neil brought Miss Joan down the diner stairs and to the plane. Dan had quickly gotten into the plane so that he could help with the transfer.

Harry hung back, not wanting to be in the way. But he stayed close enough to what was going on to be there for the woman he loved.

"Miss Joan would have a fit if she saw this plane in her parking lot," he commented to Ellie, struggling again not to let his emotions get the better of him. But it wasn't easy.

"She can take my head off once she gets well again," she told Harry with a smile. Then she gripped his hand, squeezing it. "And she *is* going to get well, Harry."

Harry nodded numbly. "I know she is," he answered even though they all knew there were no guarantees to be had.

On her way to board the plane, Zelda paused only once, eyeing the small passenger plane skeptically.

"Is this thing safe?" she asked uncertainly, the question intended for no one in particular.

"It's safer than walking there," Neil told Miss Joan's sister.

Hearing him, Ellie smiled at Neil. Given his reaction when she had flown him here from the Houston airport, he had undergone quite an about-face in attitude.

Neil and Dan were both now on the plane. Zelda had followed, reluctantly clambering on. She had taken a seat and then strapped herself in as if she expected to accidentally fall out of the plane in mid-flight if she wasn't secured.

Ellie turned her attention to Harry, silently offering to help him board the plane. But he shook his head, turning down her offer.

"I can manage," he told her. "You just concentrate on getting us there. Please."

"Consider it done," Ellie told him. Saying that, she circumvented the perimeter of the plane, making sure she had shut and secured all the doors. Satisfied, she finally got onboard herself.

"Okay, people, we're about to take off," she told her passengers. And then she looked over her shoulder at the one passenger on board who counted right now. "How's she doing?" she asked Neil, nodding toward Miss Joan.

"She'll be doing a lot better once we get her to Lincoln Memorial," Neil answered. "Did you already call it in, or whatever it is you have to do?" It occurred to him that he had no idea what the proper protocol was for bringing in a plane—or even if there was one when it came to landing it near a hospital. Some had helicopter pads on their roofs.

"I've already alerted the hospital that we're bringing in a critically ill patient and that we're flying her there on a plane, not a helicopter. They gave me instructions where to land. There'll be an ambulance meeting us there."

"An ambulance?" Zelda cried, frowning. "I

thought the whole idea was not to have to waste time driving my sister there."

"It is, but there's no place to land the plane," Ellie explained as she swiftly went over her checklist in her head one last time. "Don't worry, the landing field is half a mile from the hospital," she told Zelda then promised, "They'll have Miss Joan there in no time."

"Hope you know what you're talking about," Zelda commented, grabbing her armrests as the plane taxied the short distance and then took off.

Neil focused on his patient and not the dip in his stomach just then.

"Don't worry, Zelda. She always knows what she's talking about," he assured the woman. For just a split second, he spared Ellie a quick glance and an even quicker smile.

She didn't know what had made her do it, but she had turned around just then and caught the look that Neil gave her. There were no words to describe how that made her feel or how empowered.

She realized just how much Neil had come to mean to her in an incredibly short amount of time. She would have one hell of a time trying to come to terms with life once he went back to New York.

Now wasn't the time, she told herself.

"It's going to be all right," she promised Harry

and Miss Joan's sister, who had grown eerily quiet. "We're almost there already."

"Yeah, well, I'm not going to be happy until this flying matchbox lands in one piece," Zelda commented.

"Amen to that," Ellie thought she heard Neil murmur under his breath.

She had no idea why, but both comments made her want to laugh—but she didn't.

"Hang on, everyone. Just a few more minutes," she promised. "I can see the airfield up ahead."

"Make sure you land in it," Zelda told her sharply.

No doubt about it, Ellie thought, this woman was definitely Miss Joan's sister. She wouldn't have thought that the world had room for two Miss Joans, but obviously she had thought wrong.

## Chapter Nineteen

As she sat there in the Lincoln Memorial OR waiting room, Ellie concluded that waiting was very possibly the hardest thing in the world to do. She felt as if she had been sitting in that room an inordinate amount of time, waiting for the surgery to be over and for Miss Joan to be wheeled into Recovery.

Until that came to pass, she wouldn't be able to breathe easily.

For the most part, she and Dan had spent the time since Miss Joan had been wheeled into the OR attempting to comfort Harry and Zelda, assuring Miss Joan's husband and her sister that everything would be all right. Though he tried it hide it, Harry looked as if he was really frightened about the outcome while Zelda just appeared to be in varying states of anger.

Ellie had a feeling that if the tables had been turned, Miss Joan would have handled the situation pretty much the same way.

Ellie was also very glad that Dan had elected to remain at the hospital with everyone once Miss Joan had been taken into surgery. He was able to bring the voice of reason and common sense to the scene, helping Miss Joan's relatives cope.

Because of his familiarity with Miss Joan's condition, not to mention his rather high standing in the cardiac surgeons' community, Neil was allowed to be part of Miss Joan's surgical team. The last she had seen of him, Neil had disappeared behind the operating room doors to scrub up.

By her watch, that had been over five hours ago.

During that time, Zelda had come close to wearing a path in the tiled floor with her endless restless pacing. For the umpteenth time, the woman looked toward the doors that led into the operating room.

"Something's gone wrong and they don't want to come out to tell us," Miss Joan's sister accused nervously.

Ellie glanced at Harry, wanting to shield the man at all costs.

"Don't go there," she told Zelda, her voice sounding a great deal stricter than it normally did. "Not until we know that for a fact—and we *don't*."

Zelda opened her mouth, looking at Ellie in surprise. But then she closed it again, backing off. However she continued to look disgruntled.

"Nicely done," Dan whispered to Ellie, who was sitting next to him. "I didn't know you had it in you."

Ellie's mouth curved slightly. "Neither did I," she admitted. And then she quickly jumped to her feet when she saw the OR doors opening. Neil came into the room.

The heart surgeon was instantly surrounded by the five people in the waiting room.

"How is she?" Harry asked, clearly afraid of the answer but even more afraid of continuing to be in limbo.

Neil did his best to summarize what had gone on in layman's terms. "Miss Joan's had an angioplasty and I also performed a partial ablation. That should take care of her blockage as well as get her atrial fibrillation under control," he told Harry and Cash, who had driven to the hospital to be there for his grandfather. Neil forced a smile to his lips.

"With any luck, she should be up and about, chewing everyone out in next to no time."

Cash breathed a heavy sigh of relief.

"Heaven help me, I can't wait," Harry said. And then he surprised Neil by throwing his arms around the surgeon and hugging him with all his might. "Thank you," he cried, his voice all but breaking. "Thank you!"

Zelda nodded, although she remained where she was and didn't attempt to hug Neil. "What he said," was all the woman added.

Neil nodded, beginning to understand the way the woman operated. "Miss Joan's in Recovery now, but you can all go see her once she's out."

Suddenly feeling wiped out, Neil sank onto the closest chair. A lot of time had gone by. Beyond the hospital windows, dawn was beginning to slowly give light to the world.

Ellie changed seats, taking one next to Neil. Dan, she noticed, tactfully let them have their space, choosing to remain with Harry, Cash and Zelda.

"Can I get you anything?" she asked Neil. "Coffee? Tea? Something to eat from the vending machine—although I have to warn you, the selection is rather limited."

Neil shook his head, turning her down. "Just sit here with me and let me savor the moment."

Her mouth quirked into a quick smile. "That, I can do," Ellie responded. "I've always had a weakness for heroes."

Neil shook his head, rejecting the label. "Just doing my job."

"And being a hero," she insisted, pointing out, "It's not everyone who can ride to the rescue."

Neil was too tired at the moment to argue.

Less than ten minutes later, Cash's wife, Ramona, finally arrived. The vet had driven in following an emergency surgery of her own.

After anxiously asking about her husband's stepgrandmother, and finding out that Miss Joan had responded well to the surgeries, she hugged Cash and looked extremely relieved.

Turning to Ellie, Cash told her that he could take Harry and Zelda back with them when they were ready to leave, freeing Ellie up to leave now.

"I know that Dr. Dan probably wants to get back to the clinic and you probably need to get back, as well," he said to Neil.

"As long as you give us a ride to my plane, I can take it from there," Ellie told Cash.

Ramona glanced at her husband, noticing that some of the color was returning to Harry's face. "Is Miss Joan conscious yet?"

Zelda spoke up before Harry or Cash could. "She's still in Recovery."

Ramona nodded. "Then we have some time," she said. Cash looked at Ellie and the two physicians. "Ready whenever you are," he offered.

All three were on their feet immediately.


"Are you sure you're up to flying?" Neil asked Ellie once they had arrived at the airfield and Cash and Ramona were on their way back to the hospital.

"Don't worry," she assured him. "I can do this with my eyes closed."

"If it's all the same with you, I'd really rather you did it with your eyes open," Neil told her.

Ellie laughed. "I can do that, too," she responded with a grin. "Besides, I'm not the one who was on my feet for over five hours in the operating room, saving a life."

"Like I said, just doing my job," he told her. "Now, I know of two pretty tired men who would really be grateful if you went ahead with yours and got us back to Forever," he said, glancing at Dan. The latter merely nodded his agreement.

"Gentlemen, your chariot awaits," she told her passengers whimsically, gesturing toward the front of her plane.

\* \* \*

Compared to their flight to the hospital, the return flight seemed completely uneventful and over before it had gotten underway. Suppressing a smile, Ellie noticed that Neil hadn't turned pale even once during the trip. By the time the man was ready to go back home, he would be an old hand at this. She had no idea why that made her feel so incredibly sad, but it did.

Neil, Dan and Ellie were unprepared for the fanfare that greeted them when they finally returned to Forever. It seemed as if half the town converged around them, seemingly popping out of nowhere.

They were immediately beset with questions about Miss Joan and it felt as if everyone wanted to buy each of them celebratory drinks at Murphy's. Most of the offers were politely declined after the first one or two had been placed in front of them.

Nothing dampened the celebration, though. Everyone, it turned out, had been extremely worried that Miss Joan wouldn't make it.

The questions and impromptu celebrating didn't die down until way into the evening.

Dan never managed to get back to his clinic. To compensate, most of his patients demurred, saying that whatever had brought them to the clinic could definitely keep for at least another day if not two. The patients unable to wait were seen by Dan's associate, Dr. Cordell.

When the celebrating finally wound down and everyone began returning to their homes, Ellie turned to Neil. "I can drive you over to Dan's house," she offered. Dan and his wife had already left, but Neil had been prevailed upon to hang back awhile longer.

Instead of saying yes, Neil laced his fingers through Ellie's and suggested, "Why don't you drive us over to Dan's cabin instead? I think I've gotten my second wind."

It wasn't hard to read between the lines. Ellie smiled at him. "Oh, so I take it you still feel like celebrating?"

"You could say that, yes," Neil answered, a sexy, incredibly mischievous smile curving his mouth.

"Works for me," she told him. Walking to her vehicle, they got in and Ellie started up her Jeep. "I've always wanted to know what it felt like to be kissed by a hero."

"Oh, I intend to do a lot more than that," he told her. "And I'm not a hero," he said again. "Just a guy who was lucky enough to be in the right place at the right time."

"I don't think Miss Joan will see it that way," Ellie told him as she pulled up in front of the cabin. "Trust me, as long as you're in Forever, you're going to be on the receiving end of a whole lot of free meals at the diner."

"Then I'd better look into having some of my pants let out," he said as he unlocked the cabin door and led the way inside.

For just a moment, Ellie could feel her heart leap. But the next moment she warned herself not to read too much into Neil's words. All the surgeon was saying was that he would be here for a little bit, nothing more. He definitely didn't mean what she wished with all her heart that he meant.

Just for now, though, she decided to pretend that he did. After all, she had nothing to lose.

Neil closed the door behind him, flipping the lock and hearing it click into place.

"It occurred to me that if Miss Joan hadn't been as hearty as she was—and if you weren't there to fly all of us to the hospital, she could have easily died."

"But she was, and I was, so she didn't," Ellie said, catching her breath as Neil started undressing her.

She would really miss this when he left—

Ellie immediately upbraided herself for focusing

on negative thoughts. She needed to focus only on the good parts, she silently insisted. There would be time enough to focus on negative thoughts later.

"But what about the next time?" Neil asked.

Her pulse launched into double-time.

"Dan and Alisha will deal with that when it comes up." This wasn't where her head was at right now, she thought, responding to Neil. She started to remove his clothing. "Stop talking."

His grin was positively wicked. "All right."

For a while, he did stop talking, losing himself instead in her and glorying in the way she made him feel—as if he was ten feet tall and totally invincible.

When it was over and, shrouded in the misty afterglow of lovemaking, lying together on the gurney that they had turned into a makeshift bed, Neil returned to the subject that had been at the back of his mind for most of the day.

"Forever needs a hospital."

The statement, coming out of the blue the way it did, caught Ellie completely off guard. It took her a moment to be able to respond.

"No argument," she agreed. "Do you have a solution?" She was kidding.

But he wasn't.

"I have a trust fund," he told her.

"Sure you do," she said, nibbling on his shoulder affectionately.

She was distracting him and he wanted to get this out before he got really carried away again.

"No. I do," he told her. "I really do." What she was doing was making his eyes roll back in his head, and he needed to tell her this part so she would understand.

"I'm an only child. My parents were very well off, and add to that my mother's great-aunt—Aunt Grace—who never had any kids. She was always too busy making her money work for her and, apparently, it worked very, very hard. When she died, she left all her money to me."

Ellie pulled herself up on her elbow and looked at him, an eerie feeling that she was on the cusp of something really big emerging, though she was afraid of getting carried away. "What is it that you're saying?" she asked in a small voice.

"I'm saying that I have enough for some serious seed money to put into starting a hospital here in Forever," Neil told her. "And I honestly think I know enough people to contact who will put up the rest of it."

"You're talking about getting money together to build a hospital. Here. In Forever." Ellie didn't know if she was asking, or reiterating, as she stared at him. Being nude under the sheet didn't exactly help her thinking process, either.

"You're a little late to the party," Neil told her with a smile, "but yes, that is exactly what I'm talking about."

Ellie realized that she wasn't absorbing this. "But why?"

"Because it really hit me today that the next time someone needs an emergency operation, there might not be enough time for you to fly them to Lincoln Memorial or some other hospital. They could die because there isn't a hospital here."

"That's all well and good, but this is all going to take time," she pointed out. "Lots of time."

"I am aware of that. I was kind of good in math that way. Not brilliant," he allowed, "but good enough."

Ellie put her fingers on his lips to still them. Hope began to rise within her. "You'll have to be here at least part of the time to oversee this project, won't you?"

"Nothing gets by you, does it?" He laughed. "I will," he answered. "Probably all the time I'm not here, I'll be out there, hitting up friends for donations," Neil told her.

"Wait. Wait!" she cried, trying to get this all

straight in her head and at the same time to not get too excited because it really *couldn't* be what she thought it was—could it? She drew her courage together and forced herself to ask, "So you're staying in Forever?" Even as she asked, she braced herself for a negative answer.

"Uh-huh."

Her eyes widened. "Really?" she cried, her heart beating hard.

"Really," he echoed.

She threw her arms around his neck, kissing him soundly. She was prepared to continue and make love with him all over again, but he surprised her by catching hold of her arms and pulling them away from him.

"There's one more thing," he told her.

Ellie felt a knot suddenly materialize in the pit of her stomach, pulling tightly and somehow managing to steal all the air from her lungs. She tried to brace herself for what she felt was coming, but she knew she really couldn't.

"What?" she asked in a shaky whisper.

Holding her hand and still very naked, he slipped out of bed and down to one knee, and said, "Elliana Montenegro, will you do me the supreme honor of becoming my wife?"

She didn't know whether to laugh or cry—or get her hearing checked.

"What?" she asked, stunned.

"You don't have to change your name if you don't want to. Because yours sounds so lyrical, I understand you wanting to keep it, but I'd really be very happy if you said yes—"

"Yes!" she cried, hardly believing her ears. The man she had found herself falling in love with was actually asking her to marry him. How wonderful was that? "Yes, I'll marry you."

"Really?" he cried, surprised. "Because I thought I'd have to do a lot more convincing, or that you'd tell me you had to think about it or—"

"Please stop talking!" Ellie pleaded. "I want to start practicing for the honeymoon and I can't if you're talking."

He grinned at her, loving her so much that it actually physically hurt. "Yes, ma'am."

Neil noted, with pleasure, that her smile went all the way up into her eyes. Capturing his heart, it took him prisoner.

As did Ellie when he started kissing her again.

## *Epilogue*

Years later, whenever she talked about it, Miss Joan told people that she'd nearly had to die to bring Ellie and Neil together—but it had been worth it. The woman thought nothing of taking full credit for the young couple getting married because, in her mind, she really was the one person responsible for the two of them meeting in the first place.

When Neil and Ellie went back to Lincoln Memorial to see how the woman was doing after her surgery, even in her weakened state, the sharp-tongued diner owner only needed to take one look at the duo to discern that there was something different going on between them.

"So, what's going on, you two?" she asked in a raspy voice.

Neil took the question at face value, but Ellie wasn't so sure. This was Miss Joan asking and the woman had an eerie way of knowing things before they were ever made public.

"We're just happy that you've pulled through and are going to be all right," Ellie said, hoping that would satisfy Miss Joan's question.

She and Neil had decided to get married as soon as they found the time, but for now, they were both agreed that they wanted to hang on to this special secret just a little while longer.

"Is that your story, too, sonny?" Miss Joan asked, turning her eyes on Neil.

"Yes," he answered, doing his best to sound as innocent as possible.

Miss Joan frowned. "Look, I didn't escape the Grim Reaper's clutches just to have you two blow smoke up my butt."

Exhaling a very short breath, the woman looked at her husband, who was also in the room and hadn't left her side since she'd been brought in. "How about you, Harry? You know anything?" But even as she asked the question, Miss Joan answered for him. "No. Of course you don't. That's okay. I didn't marry you for your ability to see through people's fabrications. I married you for your sweet innocence and kind heart."

She paused to clear her throat and then continued as if nothing had happened. "You're not leaving here, you know—neither one of you—until you've come clean."

Ellie knew the woman meant it. Rather than engage in a battle of wills, she told Miss Joan, "Neil asked me to marry him."

"Yes. And?" Miss Joan asked, waiting for Ellie to get to the point.

Ellie's smile was brilliant as she answered, "And I said yes."

Miss Joan huffed. "Well, it's about damn time," she said as if the union Ellie had just told her about had been a forgone conclusion to her. "And just to prove that there are no hard feelings about you dragging Zelda back into my life, I'll be the one throwing the wedding for you two."

Because the first part of her statement was even more mind-boggling than the second part, Neil had to ask, "Wait, does that mean that you and your sister have patched things up?" Because if they had, he felt as if this was a really big deal, given the anger he had seen on Miss Joan's face the day Zelda had walked into the diner with them.

"Well, right now there's just Scotch tape, not duct tape, holding everything together, but I guess you could say that," Miss Joan allowed magnanimously. She pulled her blanket up closer around her. "I'm letting her work at the diner for now. She's on probation," she added. "We'll see how it goes."

Ellie smiled. She had a good feeling about this, she thought, exchanging glances with Neil and Harry.

"But enough about that," Miss Joan said abruptly. "I need to start making plans for your wedding. The end of the month should work..." she decided, then continued talking.

Yes, Ellie thought as the man who could create upheavals throughout her body with his mere touch reached for her hand, lacing his fingers through hers, the end of the month would definitely work for her.

\* \* \* \* \*

# WE HOPE YOU ENJOYED
# THIS BOOK FROM

## ✦H HARLEQUIN
# SPECIAL
# EDITION

*Believe in love. Overcome obstacles. Find happiness.*

Relate to finding comfort and strength in the
support of loved ones and enjoy the journey
no matter what life throws your way.

**6 NEW BOOKS AVAILABLE EVERY MONTH!**

"Sweet dreams, little one," he said and stepped out of
the room.

She took off Hannah's shoes and jeans, then tucked
her in for the night. With a bolstering breath, she braced
herself for being alone with her fantasy man.

He stood in the center of the living room, looking
around like he'd never seen his own house. She
followed Anson's gaze to the built-in shelves she'd
filled with precious and painful memories. Things she
wasn't ready to share with him. Before he could ask any
questions, she opened the front door.

"Even though we were coerced, thank you for carrying her home. And for the house tour." Their "moment" in his bedroom flashed before her. *Damn, why'd I bring that up?*

"Anytime." Anson's blue-eyed gaze danced with amusement before he ducked his head and stepped outside. "Sleep well, Tess."

Fat chance of that.

She closed the door to prevent herself from watching him walk away. Tonight, Anson hadn't treated her indifferently like before and, in fact, seemed to be fighting his own temptations. Sometimes shutters would fall over his eyes as he distanced himself, then she'd blink and he'd wear his devil's grin, drawing her in with flirtation. Maybe he wasn't as immune to their attraction as she'd thought.

"I can't figure you out, Chief Anson Curry. But why am I even bothering?"

*Don't miss*
A Sheriff's Star *by Makenna Lee,*
*available November 2020 wherever*
*Harlequin Special Edition books and ebooks are sold.*

Harlequin.com